Runaways

A Novel

Doug Lambeth

Sashee Press
Pullman, Washington

Published by:

Sashee Press

Pullman, WA

ISBN 978-0-9728-2184-1

Ard1651@hotmail.com

Additional copies are available at: www.lulu.com

Runaways

Scooter

Chapter One

"I don't love you anymore."

My spoonful of Cheerios hovers right below my mouth. I suppose I shouldn't, but I go ahead and shovel them in. Big mistake, because as Jane's words hit I'm soon hawking and gagging Safeway nonfat and Cheeri-oat fragments all over the table.

"I'm running away with Dr. Dwayne," she continues.

"Our periodontist?" I croak, milk dribbling down my chin. I've never seen Dr. Dwayne's mouth; he always wears a mask while he hacks away at my gums. But now, as I think of it, I sensed a smirk below the mask during my last visit. And I thought he was just contemptuous because he knew I hadn't been flossing.

"He's an exciting, stimulating man," Jane adds, loading her purse with supermarket coupons from the kitchen junk drawer.

"Are you going to the store?"

"Yes."

"I need deodorant," I say.

Jane sighs tiredly. Apparently, she finds me dull. I suppose exciting, stimulating Dr. Dwayne doesn't wear deodorant. "This will be the last time," Jane sighs again.

"For what?"

"Getting your deodorant." She gives me a long, sad look. "Sorry, Scooter."

"Don't call me Scooter."

"I thought you liked the name?"

"Not anymore. It's a little kid name." I sound surly to myself, but I can't help it. My wife has just announced she's running off with a guy who slices gums for a living. And *that's* exciting to her.

Which means I must be *really* boring.

"We'll talk more later, but you need to know, Scoot—Jimmy, I get Crystal. You can have her for a week during the summer and alternating Christmases. My attorney said I could press it if I have to. Since you haven't been that interested in her at all."

"You've talked to a lawyer already?" I ask, more upset by that than the fact that she's planning on estranging me from my own daughter. I don't know why. I guess I've been a lousy father. But I've never been able to warm up to the kid—she's seven and sullen and sulky and a lot like her mother.

"Dr. Dwayne's lawyer. He's got everything written up. As soon as you hire your own lawyer he'll send it over for you to sign. You'll find it more than fair."

"How can you be so...."

"Cold?"

"Yeah. And calculating."

"I read a book. I'm empowered."

"By Dr. Dwayne's dick."

"Don't be crude. It's over, Jimmy. Accept it. Get on with your life."

Jane has never looked tougher. She's like a middle linebacker zeroing in on a hapless QB, relishing the thought of hitting him low and blowing out his ACL. A cold milk dribble dangles on my chin and then drips on the table. But I don't wipe it off. I'm too stunned.

"You'll be fine," Jane says, heading out the door. "I'll see you tonight. I'll help you pack your stuff. And I'll pick Crystal up from school. Bye."

And with that she's gone. Amazing. She's acting like *all* she's doing is running to the store—not torpedoing my life. It's weird, though...just now, as she was heading out the door and kicking me in the figurative crotch, she's never looked better. Jane's not an ultra-model-babe or anything—she's one of those "attractive" women—whatever that means. But now, clutching her purse full of coupons for orange juice and tampons, she was like Xena, The Warrior Princess, ballcrushingly scary but sexually alluring. Great. I've been a little distant, maybe a little less than sexually attentive lately, and now, the second my wife tells me she's dumping me for a periodontist, I'm horny.

God's sure got a weird-ass sense of humor.

I grab the phone. As it touches my chin, the cold milk film smears the mouthpiece. I don't care. I need to talk to Erica.

I'm sitting in Eric and Erica's cluttered living room. Toys litter the threadbare carpet, scattered randomly like those pictures you see after the tornado pulverizes the trailer park in Alabama. Battered Barbies, disemboweled G.I. Joes that look like they stepped on landmines, electronic game guts—all the detritus of seven home-schooled, rowdy kids. Eric and Erica started breeding early and often, and by the time Erica hit thirty-two she was the proud mother of six towheaded demons from hell. She stopped for a few years, and then little Eli came along as an exclamation point. The oldest girl, Elizabeth, helps Erica out with the feeding and educating, but she's planning to head off to some bible college next year. Poor Erica. She'll be stuck with the rest of them for years to come. So many rugrats. Don't get me wrong, they're cute kids and all, but seven of anything is too much. Especially if you have to feed them.

"Doctor Dwayne?!" Erica says, her mouth spitting Doctor Dwayne's name out like it's a turd-filled bonbon. Ezekial, her six-and-a-half-year-old, runs shrieking into the living room chased by Boomer, their Corgi. Boomer likes to herd the little kids. He nips at Eli's diaper and pulls it down half-mast. "Just a second," Erica sighs, exasperation and exhaustion flopping over her face like a limp dishrag. Poor Erica. My all-time best buddy, the woman I should've married, reduced to breeding, home-schooling, and chasing Corgis and towheaded kids whose names all start with "E". She follows them out into the kitchen, and I hear her scolding Ezekial for not keeping on eye on Eli, and then she yells at Elishaba and Elizabeth to get busy studying the bible passages they're supposed to memorize.

Erica and I were band fags in high school. She played the tuba, I pounded spastically on the bass drum. We wore the geeky uniforms and marched in sad little formations during football game halftimes, either ignored or insulted by the fans. Eric was the QB, the ultimate stud, and when Erica caught his eye—because for a band fag she was awfully cute, even in her ridiculously towering feather-topped hat and pearl white tuba—he pursued her relentlessly. Any thought I might have had at having Erica for myself—which never occurred to me until Eric went after her—disappeared with Eric's broken field scrambling pursuit. He had quick feet, and he bagged her in no time. He would've been a great linebacker.

They got married the day after high school graduation, and then the babies started arriving with biennial regularity. For some reason she'd always get pregnant in the summer, and invariably deliver in late February; I told her she should name her kids permutations of George.

Eric went to work in his family's beer distributorship right out of high school. He'd wanted to play college ball, but his dad, the ultimate hard-ass "I didn't need no college and neither do you" kind of guy made him work. Probably just as well; with all the babies, Eric would've had a hard time memorizing X's and O's.

When a pallet full of pony kegs tipped off a forklift and crushed his dad in a foamy cascade of Budweiser, Eric saw Jesus. He became born again—because you never knew when Jesus would call you home in a tidal wave of Bud—and he dragged Erica along with him. She loved him with all her heart and soul, but I know she has never bought into the holy-roller stuff. She's too smart and too cynical to be a bible thumper, but she goes along.

Good old Erica.

I wish to hell I'd married her instead of Jane.

She finally comes back into the living room, kicking an armless Prom Queen Barbie out of the way.

"Sorry, Scooter," she sighs, plopping down on the couch next to me. "These damn kids...."

"Would you ever leave Eric?" I ask. I don't know why.

"Of course not. I love him."

"What if you fell in love with somebody else. Like a periodontist or something."

"Nope. Wouldn't be right. I mean, if Eric were bad to me or the kids, maybe. But I made a deal, a commitment, and as long as he keeps his end of the deal, I keep mine."

"I shoulda married you," I say miserably.

She touches my hand with surprising tenderness but says nothing. You have to understand something about me and Erica; we're pals, the way most guys are pals. I've never kissed her, except for a clumsy peck on the cheek the day she got married. But we've been buds, confidants, everything you look for and are lucky to get in a best friend but never seem to be able to find in a spouse.

We met freshman year, right after I got cut from the football team. I'd tried out for a lineman spot, because although I was a klutzy dork I was big; but size couldn't overcome geekiness, and when the coach posted the names of the loser spazzes who didn't make the team, I was secretly relieved. I'd already gotten thumped pretty good in two-a-days, and I knew that if I'd made the team the only position I'd have been any good at was a living tackling dummy.

The afternoon I got cut I was leaning against the side of the gym, waiting for a buddy who made the team to give me a ride. I felt both self-pity and relief. I must've looked pretty forlorn and pathetic, because Erica wandered over from a cluster of girls waiting for their rides.

"Hi," she said.

"Hi," I said. I knew vaguely who she was. We were in Algebra I together, although we'd never spoken.

"Did you make the team?" she asked.

"How did you know I was trying out for the team?" I asked. I looked at her for the first time. She was all gawky elbows and knees and freckles and braces; but still, that first time I really looked at her, there was something about the hell-raiser smile, the too-smart twinkle in her eye, that made me like her. Not as a girl, mind you. But as a bud.

"I've seen you out there. You aren't very good. All the big guys were crushing you."

"Yeah. That's why I didn't make the team."

"Too bad."

"Not really."

"Why?" she asked.

"Because I'm kind of a pussy."

She laughed at that. And then we were friends. She talked me into joining the marching band; I'd never touched a bass drum in my life, but she gave me a cram course and the band director, who was in dire need of bodies, let me join. So I marched and *boom-boom-boomed* my way through high school and Erica was my best friend.

My only friend.

That's the weird thing. I never hung out with guys. I knew them, but I never did anything with *The Guys*. Only Erica. And as she grew up, and the braces came off and the breasts popped out, suddenly my best pal was a very pretty, fine-looking young thing.

But I didn't do anything about it.

Because we were just friends.

Everybody in high school assumed we were a couple; it was a natural assumption since we were always together. But they should've noticed there was never any of that clingy stuff between us, the "IloveyousomuchI-can'tletgoofyouevenforaminute" that you saw the *real* pairs doing. We just laughed and scratched and made fun of the world and were friends. And then Eric bagged her and things changed.

Eric's a good guy. He always understood my friendship with Erica; probably it didn't bother him that his girlfriend and wife-to-be's best pal was a guy because he thought I was gay. So did a lot of people after he hooked up with Erica.

I asked other girls out, trying to get over the irritation of being branded a rump-ranger, but nothing interesting ever came of it. And I didn't start hanging with guys, because if you haven't hooked up with pals by the time you're a junior in high school, you never will.

So I ended up in sort of third-wheel limbo land with Eric and Erica. I went on a lot of dates with them...I know, it's relentlessly weird, but that's how things worked out. Eric didn't mind, and Erica expected it, so we ended up as a strange little trio.

But it was because of Eric hooking up with Erica that I found my career. Hanging out with Eric, I heard lots of insider stories about the football team and the coaches, and I realized that I wanted to be part of sports somehow. Since I was too much of a pussy to play, and I didn't want to be an ultimate loser like a team manager or something dorky like that, I decided I'd write about it. I got into the school newspaper, discovered I knew how to write, and before I knew what had happened, I was the head sports reporter for the Weekly Trojan. And after high school, while Eric and Erica were breeding, I went to college, got a journalism degree, met and married Jane, moved back to the home town, and ended up with a job as Jimmy "Scooter" Biffman, lead sports ace with *The Daily Reporter*, specializing in coverage of high school athletics in the tri-county area. Life was good.

Until a little while ago, when Jane decided to dump me for Dr. Dwayne.

Erica's hand rests gently on mine. "Scooter," she whispers. "I'm so sorry."

I look at her. All the years, all the kids, the diapers, the bible readings, everything, but she's still the same cute little braces-and-elbows kid who was my best pal. *Is* my best pal.

My heart races. It's pounding. Oh shit...am I having a coronary?! I'm only forty, for Christ's sake, too young to be checking out. What're the symptoms, your jaw's supposed to hurt, isn't it? And what about your arm? One of your arms is supposed to ache or something.

"Scooter?" Erica asks. "What's wrong?"

"Gasping...."

Erica expertly smacks me on the back. Something about the painful whack knocks me back into the now and my massive myocardial infarction symptoms disappear as suddenly as they appeared.

"There. Sometimes when Ezekial gets panicky all I need to do is get his attention off himself and he's back to normal in no time."

"Panic? I was having a panic attack?"

"Scoot, Jane dumped you for Dr. Dwayne. You're entitled."

"Jane dumped me."

"I never liked her, to tell you the truth."

"No shit, Er. You were the only person I danced with at our wedding who told me my new wife was Hitler with breasts."

"I was right, too. I should've used a more vivid description. Like the 'C' word."

"Be nice. What would Eric think if he heard you talking like this?"

"Pray, I suppose," she sighs. Erica gets weary of the holy stuff. It's not her style.

I flop back against the couch. Yowling kids fight out in the family room, and Erica will soon have to go and referee her litter. I'm just an annoyance, I know. Even though we're best buds, it's not like she can do a whole lot.

Except....

"I need someplace to stay. She's kicking me out."

Erica stands, heading out to discipline somebody whose name begins with "E". "Eric will be home in a little while. We'll talk. I think there's space in the trailer. If that's okay."

"Sure. Great."

Erica gives me a sad, tired smile and vanishes into the kitchen. Kids start to yowl, in anticipation of their chewing-out. I sit on the couch. I feel heavy, like I've gained fifty pounds in the last couple of hours. I want to eat; plates of spaghetti, Doritos, Pop-Tarts, Cadbury Eggs (if only it were Easter), beer, something, anything....

This is it. The first step of depression. Ultimate munchies, like you've been smoking pot for a week.

I'm gonna be fat and alone and living in Eric and Erica's trailer the rest of my life.

Fucking Jane.

I realize suddenly that I've never really cared for her.

Erica was right.

She's a...I can't bring myself to think it. But she's a "C"-word.

"May the peace of our Lord and Savior Jesus Christ come upon you and give you his peaceful salvation. May His peace give you peace. May your peace come from His peace. Amen."

"AMEN!" all the "E" kids respond to Eric's prayer. I'm still trying to get all the "peace's" straight as Erica dishes up savory slices of oatmeal-extended meatloaf and a massive pan of Stovetop Stuffing. She and Eric have a hard time making ends meet, since Erica stays home to breed and home school, and the money Eric makes is good but only goes so far with such a crowd. The only perk of his job is beer, but he doesn't drink and neither do the kids, so what good is it? Erica called Eric and gave him a heads-up what was going on with me, and being the good guy that he is, Eric brought home a couple of expired Michelobs. Eric's real thoughtful for a born-again guy.

We eat, but there isn't much normal conversation. With the massive crowd of kids, there's always a spill, a fight, tears, something. Eric and Erica must have terminal indigestion; by the time dinner's over all the squabbling has left me frazzled and nervous. Eric leads me out to the living room to have another beer while Erica and Elizabeth and the rest of the "E" girls clean up. That's the way things are in this house—females do women's work and men don't. The boys wander off to study and fight over who gets to use the one computer. I don't know how a house full of kids can survive with only one computer these days.

It's strange. Eric's a together guy, always has been, but I'll bet he can't boil water or turn on the washing machine. First his mom took care of him, then Erica. I'll never understand guys who are proud of being helpless. Maybe that was part of the problem in my marriage; I did everything, from cleaning the toilets to changing Crystal's diapers to sautéing onions for recipes.

It occurs to me with the sudden certainty of all-knowing clarity...Jane took advantage of me. I was whipped.

Eric shuffles painfully bow-legged ahead of me. He's aging quickly. He moves like John Elway right after he retired. I sit on the couch—moving broken toys—and suddenly Eric is in front of me, putting his hands on my head. I know what's coming.

"Oh, most heavenly Father, give your son Scooter the strength to persevere through the troubled times that lie ahead. Fill him with love and peace. Amen."

"Amen," I say, not so much that I'm into the praying, because at this point in my life I'm not sure there's any supreme being except maybe for Springsteen and Elvis, but Elvis is dead so he doesn't count. Eric rests his hands on my head longer than he needs to; I want him to finish up so I can get back to chugging my warm, flat Michelob. He's whispering some holy mumbo-jumbo, and I'm having a hard time remembering the studly football player he once was. Now he's tired and pasty. I've noticed that about religious people...the color drains from their skin. Why is that? A sinning scumbag has nice healthy-looking skin. I look down at my hands. They're tanned and healthy. Obviously no holiness here.

Eric finally wraps up the praying and creaks into the battered La-Z-Boy like he's a hundred years old.

"You need to get those knees scoped, Eric. You're gonna be walking like Frankenstein pretty soon."

"I know," he sighs. "Can't afford the time off right now. Business isn't as good as it could be." Eric doesn't often talk about work because he hates it. He knows he's trapped. What a shame. We all start off our lives with such high hopes, but it seems like for 99.9% of us, things end up shitty.

"Er ask you about the trailer?" I ask. The thought of living in their beat-up Airstream in the back yard is less than appealing, but I'm short of dough and it's probably only going to get worse with lawyers and all, and at least here I'll be close to the only friends I have in the world.

"Yeah, it's fine, Scoot. I'll run an extension cord out to it, and the hose. Be good as gold." Eric sighs; he looks at me, and his eyebrows knit into an odd shape, kind of like he's surprised, scared and amused all rolled into one.

"What?" I ask.

He doesn't say anything for a long moment. Eric's still a good-looking guy, craggy and manly, and the age creases beginning to sneak into the hollows below his eyes only accentuate his attractiveness. I hate to sound like a fag, but he's still a stud. I bet he fends off women all the time, unless his Jesus armor is so strong that they don't even bother.

"I'm...." he starts to say, his voice really quiet and raspy.

"What?" I ask, expecting some more "Heavenly Father bless you" stuff.

"I'm...really...happy for you," he says, and the sudden tortured look on his face, the shock and horror is such that it's like he just said he loves Satan or something.

Still, it *is* an odd thing to say to a guy whose wife dumped him a few hours before.

"Whatcha mean, Eric?" I ask lightly, trying to soften the big leaden turd his weird statement just dropped into the room.

"I mean," he says, struggling for the right words. "I mean that you're free."

"I guess you could say that," I say. "If that kind of freedom is good."

"I envy you," he whispers, his eyes darting to the door.

Oh shit.... There's trouble here, trouble I never noticed. I thought Eric and Erica were solid, that they were the one constant I could always count on: Eric and Erica, in love and dropping babies till the day Erica started menopause or Eric couldn't get it up anymore.

"Oh man," I moan. "Don't tell me this, Eric. I've had enough shitty news for one day."

"No, no, no, it's not like that!" he says desperately. "I'm not...interested in going the same way."

"Then what the hell are you talking about?" I ask, feeling sudden loyalty to Erica surge through me. Eric's my pal, but Erica was there first; she's the one who really counts.

He rubs his eyes and puts his head in his hands. "I don't know," he says. "Forget it. Forget what I said."

And then he quickly gets up, mumbling prayers, and does his hobbling hopalong shuffle out of the room.

The Michelob tastes sour. I hope expired beer doesn't have botulism in it or something....

"Hi Crystal," I say. I'm talking to the back of her head as she surfs the net. The kid is computer obsessed; I realize that I have no idea where she surfs or who she's talking to online. I suppose I should've kept a closer eye on it, but for some reason I never got around to it. For all I know she's hanging out in chat rooms with Ted Bundy wannabes.

She doesn't answer, so I move closer and try again. "Hi, Crystal."

"I'm busy," she snaps. Now I know why I haven't spent much time with her. She's crabby and annoying. She takes after Jane.

But this is important, and I can't let my negativity toward her get in the way of fatherly duties, so I sit on her bed and study her profile in the computer screen's glow. She's awfully cute, pug nose and long blonde hair. She already has nasty little boys pursuing her; her teen years are going to be a nightmare, especially if her attitude gets any worse and she gets any cuter.

"Has your mom told you—"

"That she kicked you out? Yes."

"Oh." She said it so matter-of-factly that it hit me like a Randy Johnson fastball in the scrotum. "Are you okay?"

"Yes!" she snaps, but it's not because she's upset that I'm leaving. It's because I'm bugging her while she tries to surf. I decide to put this off for awhile—maybe forever, who knows.

"Okay, if you want to talk, I'll be around. I'm going to stay with Eric and Erica for awhile," I say.

"Whatever."

As I leave her room I'm torn. She *is* my daughter, and no matter how much she's...indifferent to me, I still love her. Desperately. But I don't like her, and the thought of leaving her and Jane doesn't bother me nearly as much as it should.

I pack my clothes and bathroom stuff. Jane's watching *Entertainment Tonight* and isn't interested. As I leave I say, "I'll come by on the weekend and get the rest of my stuff."

"Fine," Jane says, not unkindly. Just disinterestedly. She's so enraptured by a story about Brittney Spears that she can't be bothered to look at me.

"Fine," I say. There's nothing else to say, I suppose, but I do anyway. "I hope it wasn't always bad for you," I blurt. I don't know why. Looking for some human kindness or reassurance, I suppose.

She doesn't look away from Brittney. "What?"

"Never mind."

The walk out the front door, down the lumpy cement path I poured a couple of years ago in a fit of frenzied home improvement, the shuffle to my beat-up Camry in the driveway, is the longest, saddest walk I've ever made. I'm leaving what I know—it wasn't perfect, but what is?—for the unknown. Time in Eric and Erica's trailer, and then what? Suddenly single. Will I hang out in bars? I don't know how to meet women...it's not like I ever had much practice. Maybe I should just stay alone; I'm forty, the gut's starting to swell, the forehead's headed north, how am I going to attract women anyway?

I slam the Camry's trunk after I throw my meager belongings inside. Fourteen years of marriage, over, *poof!*, that's it. I get to start all over.

I'm inside the car now, don't remember getting in. Drop my keys on the floor, don't pick them up, staring at my ex-home, my ex-life, ex-wife, ex-daughter.

And before I realize what's happening, I'm weeping, big honking snorts, I don't usually cry but I can't stop, Jesus, what's happening to my life, I'm finished, I don't know what I'm going to do, but I've reached the bottom, things can't get any worse, and—

"We're gonna have to let you go, Scooter," Louise says.

The blood drains from my body and pools in my feet; if I tried to stand up I'd pass out. "What?" I gasp.

Louise grimaces. She's a nice lady for a boss, a few years older than me and the first female managing editor *The Daily Report* has ever had. She's one of those do-everything women—mom, over-achiever boss, climbing the ladder, active in local politics, cooks, sews...I don't know how she has time for anything. And to top it off, she's really a good, decent person. In fact, right now, while I sit in her office as she fires me, the tears are in her eyes, not mine.

"What?!" I say again, this time with some vocal cords.

"We've been bought. American News."

"American News?! They're...evil!" Maybe an overstatement, but not by much. American News is a conglomerate company that buys up small and mid-size papers, guts them, and runs *USA Today*-style mush.

"Yeah. But you know how they are. They don't value local news. Particularly local sports. I'm sorry, Scooter. I really am." She reaches for a Kleenex; I expect her to offer it to me, but instead she's wiping her own eyes, and blowing honking tear-snot. Louise is a good person to be fired by; at least you feel wanted while you're being kicked out the door.

"Is there any chance...they'll reconsider?" I ask.

"No. I'll be honest with you, Scooter, I'm probably gonna get canned before the week is out. They just want me to do the dirty work before they bring in their own stooge."

I look out through her glass-walled office. My colleagues work diligently in front of their computers. "How many are getting...laid off?" I ask. I can't bear to say the word "fired".

"Over half."

"And I'm the first?"

"Yeah."

"Thanks. I guess."

We both laugh bitterly. That stops Louise's tears. It's a good thing; she's going to be crying a lot before this blood bath is over.

"You'll land on your feet, Scooter. You've got too much talent."

"Thanks. This just comes at a bad time. Jane left me for our periodontist yesterday."

I shouldn't have told her that, because here come the tears again. "Oh Jesus, Scooter, that's terrible! I'm so sorry."

I shrug. The shotgun blast shock effect is wearing off already, and I'm thinking ahead. "Life sucks, Louise."

"Will you stay in the area?"

"I dunno. I'm living in a friend's trailer for the time being."

"You know that whatever I can do to help, career or otherwise, I'm here for you. Or somewhere, after *I* get fired," she laughs uncertainly.

"You're the best, Louise. I mean that. But I don't know what I'll do. Guess I'll update the resume and put a personal ad in the paper. How 'bout something like, 'Unemployed local sports reporter, seeking rich Cindy Crawford lookalike. Am willing to cook and clean. Will provide sexual favors as needed'."

"I'd work on it a little," she smiles. "It's kind of overwritten." A sniff, but the tear valve is off again. Good.

We chitchat a little, but I sense it's time to go. She hands me a check for a month's severance—which amazes me, since American News is notoriously cheap—and when I walk out of her office I'm officially unemployed. I was planning on interviewing Coach Kowalski over at St. Anthony's and doing an in-depth on a retarded kid who kicks field goals for the Kennedy Trojans, but now that's all history. It's going to be a thin edition of the paper tonight; I suppose it'll be filled up with junky wire service crap and bland features and not a word of local news. I watch as Ed, who covers the city desk and edits the entertainment section, trudges into Louise's office. She's already yanking Kleenex, and I feel sorry for both of them. But this is history to me now, and I've never been real close to anybody here, so I surreptitiously empty the few personal possessions in my desk into an empty Xerox paper box, and I'm gone without a word.

Now what? I drive aimlessly through town, get on the freeway and just drive. Nowhere, no purpose. Nothing to do, nobody to see, nobody who cares. Well, not entirely. Eric and Erica care. But they have their lives; I can't be too much of a bother to them. I've got to start out on my own, remake Jimmy "Scooter" Biffman.

But how?

Chapter Two

“Tough forty-eight hours,” Erica says, sipping a Kool-Aid. I know she’d rather be having a beer—she could pound the brewskies in high school before Eric decreed holy prohibition—and as we sit on saggy lawn chairs in their toy-cluttered back yard, our feet resting in the thin, scratchy lawn, I find myself again wondering—

How would things have changed if I’d only hooked up with Erica, if I’d beaten Eric to the punch. Who knows what might’ve been?

“Stop thinking about it,” Erica says. She has the creepy ability to read my mind sometimes, but I can’t imagine she’s zeroed in on this thought.

“So what am I thinking about?” I ask.

“Me.”

I gulp my Kool-Aid.

Creepy.

We silently watch the sun set over the ratty wooden fence. Its last rays reflect weakly on the polished surface of their Airstream...my new home.

Kids make noise in the house, but Eric is ringmaster for the evening. When he heard I got canned, he figured I'd need some alone time with Erica...Eric's the best. Although his cryptic "You're lucky" statement still worries me. I wonder what exactly he was talking about?

Mosquitoes buzz around my head, and Erica impatiently swats at the air. "It's almost biblical, you know?" she says, looking into her palm. She caught and squashed a mosquito in mid-buzz. I've never been able to do that.

"What?"

"What's happening to you. You're on your way to being like...fucking Job or something," she giggles. Eric frowns on foul language, and I think Erica gets a little coochie buzz out of saying "fuck" in a sentence about the bible. *Rebel, rebel.*

"Refresh me. Who's fucking Job?" I ask. My bible junk is rusty, not that it was ever very coherent.

"God kept throwing trouble at him."

"What'd he do about it?"

"Took it like guys in the Old Testament are supposed to. Bitched and moaned but in the end appreciated God for kicking his ass." Erica sips her Kool-Aid and giggles again. "Fucking Job."

She must've slipped some vodka in her Kool-Aid when Eric wasn't looking.

"Thanks. Nothing like Old Testament ass-whuppin' to make you feel like a million bucks. Am I gonna get boils, maybe some kind of plague?"

"At the rate things are going I wouldn't count it out."

"I'll make sure to share with you."

"That's not how it works. God only throws the nasty stuff at people who can take it. At least that's what Eric says."

I usually like to banter and shoot the shit with Erica, but I'm not in the mood tonight. It's my life she's joking about, and I'm suddenly not finding very much funny.

"You should write a book," Erica blurts out, giggling again. I'm sure she's been drinking. I wonder where she stashes her booze?

"About what? High school sports in the tri-county area? I don't think it'd be a best seller."

"Okay, something else. You can write. There must be something you can write about."

"My autobiography. 'Portrait of a Fucked-Up Loser'."

"Yeah. No. Too much of a downer. Something happier."

A mosquito drills my neck. I'd swat it, but why bother? There'll just be others. Jesus, listen to me. I've really given up. I swat it. I feel the satisfying blood-splat as I squash it against my skin. Okay, Scooter shows some spunk. He killed a bug. The first positive thing that's happened in the last two days.

"I don't have anything happy to write about, Erica. It's a dopey idea."

But Erica's not listening. She's staring into the indigo-smudged dusk sky, like she's waiting for a shooting star to swoosh by at any moment. "No...no I've got an idea!" she says breathlessly.

"What?"

"Write about what happens."

"To who?"

"You!"

She turns to me, full goofy grin and twinkly eyes. I haven't seen her this excited in a long time. The years of babies and diapers and "Praise Jesus" have drained away—this is the Erica I knew way back when, when we were kids.

"You mean a diary?" I ask.

"Kind of."

"That's boring, Er. What am I gonna write, 'Got up, shaved, drove around, looked for a job'...nobody cares."

"Sure, you put it like that, it's boring. But if you write it...cool, put in tension, then it's great."

"What tension?"

And now her grin gets really big. "Sexual."

"Are you nuts? Write about whacking off?"

"That'd be gross," she says, looking at me like I'm a perv. "I'm talking about the Jimmy "Scooter" Biffman search for the perfect woman. Everybody loves a love story, and everybody wants to see the nice guy win. So go find the perfect woman, the replacement for dragon Jane."

Now, I admit that at this very moment, in this very place, I'm in kind of a bad psychological state. I'm not big into all the self-analysis garbage that seems to be a lot of people's only reason for living; I take things as they come and hope for the best. But right now, out in the backyard, being eaten by skeeters and wondering if Erica is drunk or crazy or both, I have to admit that something about her notion intrigues me.

"The Scooter quest for love."

"Yeah!"

"It's kind of early for that, isn't it? Jane only dumped me yesterday."

"All the more reason to start now. The hurt's fresh, and you sure don't want her back. It's not like a big love affair blew up or something. She's a loser. Now you go out and find the right one. And write about it, make it funny. You're funny, people will want to read it."

It's stupid, ridiculous, absurd.

But I'm intrigued....

"I still need to work, though."

"Cash in your 401K."

I've got seventy-five grand in my 401K, but the thought of liquidating it to do some bonehead blue sky deal woman hunt is too much.

Still....

"What if there's no end? What if I don't find anybody?" I ask.

"Then...." Erica sips the Kool-Aid dregs and licks the edge of the glass. "Then I'll provide the happy ending."

I don't know how long mosquitoes' drill-tongues are, but by the jolting shudder that passes through my body I think one punctured my spinal cord.

"Erica!"

She doesn't say anything; she just tosses me a flirty grin.

"Er, I don't know what's going on with you and Eric, but don't be talking like that."

"Why not?" she says. "I'm bored. We're bored. He'd never say anything, but I know he feels the same way."

Actually, he *would* say something. But I don't tell her that. "No he doesn't. No you don't. You guys love each other more than anything in the world, you two are solid, you're dependable."

"We're boring."

"So what?! There's nothing wrong with boring."

"Apparently Jane thought so."

"Jane's not you. She's—"

"Satan."

I sigh. What the hell is going on? Has everybody lost their fucking minds? So I say, "Have you lost your fucking mind?!"

Erica throws her head back and laughs deeply. Her voice has gotten husky over the years. Her laugh sounds like one of those old ladies who smoke too much and have their reading glasses dangling on jeweled chains around their chicken skin necks. "This is it, Scoot. Your chance to do what everybody who's trapped wants to do! You can hit the road, crank up the stereo, go find the woman of your dreams."

"This is crazy!" I'm starting to get mad.

"No it's not, it's real. It's life we can live vicariously through you."

"You won't provide the happy ending," I huff.

"You're such a dork," she laughs.

"Promise me you won't provide a happy ending!" I say, and as the words leave my mouth I realize how idiotic they are. If I was honest I'd admit I've always wanted Erica, and the thought of finally being with her is tantalizing. Even if Eric and the kids....

Stop it! What am I thinking?! Too much stress.

"So you gonna do it?" Erica asks.

"No!"

She starts to sing *Born To Be Wild.* I try to be pissed off, but I can't, so I laugh with her. I can't help it. Everything is too absurd right now to be upset about anything.

"So where do I look for the new Ms. Right? Bars?" I ask.

Erica leans back in the chair, runs her hands through her curly hair. Damn, she's still cute.

"No. You don't want big-haired trailer trash slobs. For this to be any good you've got to have a noble quest. You've got to look for her in a place that makes sense, that we want to read about. But it's a good question. Hmmm."

She sounds like an editor. But the journalist in me can't stop thinking about it. Maybe, just maybe....

"Is there someplace where guys my age can go on a love quest without the accompanying sleaze factor?" Maybe a college campus. Lots of potential there. The only problem is that I'd be laughed out of the universe by a bunch of hard-bodied twenty-two-year-olds.

Erica "hhmmmms" thoughtfully. I'm suddenly off in fantasy land thinking about sorority babes-o-rama. Not gonna happen.

"I think," Erica says, "that you should look backward instead of forward."

"What are you, a fucking fortune cookie?"

She smiles like a Buddha.

"She was hot," Eric says, drooling over a picture of Heather McAndrews with a little more enthusiasm than I think is healthy. The three of us are on the couch poring over pictures from our high school yearbooks. This was Erica's brilliant "look backward" idea: hunt down the high school babes o' the past and try to bag one.

"But they're all probably married, Erica," I objected. "It's been twenty years."

"People get divorced. Look at you. And maybe if you're charming enough they'll leave their husband for you! What a great ending that would make!"

"Yeah, just what I want to be, a home-wrecking sleazeball."

But Erica prevailed, and before I knew it, we'd parked on the couch with Eric—who for some reason thought it was a great idea—and now I'm taking a trip down memory lane, looking at pictures of incredibly young people with bad hair.

My people. My past.

"What about Cindy?" Erica asks. We gaze down at the senior portrait of Cindy Alvarado. I smile at the memory of her tight butt. I spent a lot of time leering at her.

"Don't think we ever spoke," I say, regretting it. I didn't know at the time that looks were less important to women than personality. It's all about attitude. Wish I'd realized that when I was sixteen. I might've had a whole lot more fun than pining after Erica and flogging my crowbar raw during my nightly excursions to the land of buxom, wanton fantasy women who wanted me only as their meat boy.

Erica scribbles Cindy's name down on the ever-growing list. "You can talk to her now. It'll be great, looking all these people up."

"I'll never find them," I say, already regretting that I let Erica start this. The more she gets into it, the stupider it seems.

"That'll be my job. And the kids. They know their way around the web like nobody's business. We'll find these people."

"Great," I say weakly.

"This is so cool!" Eric says. He's way more into this than I am. And that's when it hits me. It's why this idiot idea might be worth something...because Eric's the kind of person that might actually want to read something like this. The vicarious search of an almost-middle-aged loser for a babe from the past.

Who hasn't wondered if they could fire something up with that hot blonde from second period algebra? It's why they have high school reunions—so people can get that little buzz of seeing the past and wonder...what might have been?

I didn't go to our reunions. I didn't see any reason to. There wasn't anyone I cared to see—Eric and Erica were the only high-schoolers I cared about—and anyway, Eric and Erica went and filled me in. They told me about the balding slobs and flabby girls and....

"How many of these women have you seen at the reunions?" I ask.

"A few," Erica says. "But it's weird. Most of the ones we're picking out weren't there."

"Probably because they're in prison," I say miserably. "I don't know about this," I add, the doubt blowing away my momentary "Hey, this isn't such a bad idea!"

"Quit whining," Erica orders. She's in her take-charge mode. I haven't seen it much since she started breeding—unless it was directed at the kids. To Eric, and even me, she's become deferential. This crazy idea is changing her in a hurry.

"Forget it, Erica, I'm not gonna do this," I say, starting to stand up. I'm shocked at the iron grip that locks onto my wrist and pulls me back down to the couch. It's not Eric; it's Erica.

And she's not smiling.

"You need to do this," she says through clenched teeth. "It's important."

"To who?" I ask.

"Everybody," Eric answers. And Erica nods.

What the fuck is going on with these people? Is this some sort of sick and twisted thing with them, like a perverted three-way that they've always dreamed about or something?

"You need to heal," Erica says. "You've been wounded."

"Maybe time would be a better idea than hunting for a new woman," I say. "Don't most people take more than forty-eight hours to get over huge life-changing things like marriages going tits up and jobs being yanked?"

But they're not listening. Erica's already writing another name down on her list, and Eric points at a picture. "Hey," Eric smiles. "What about Adonna Moore?"

And it's weird...hearing the name of a girl I hadn't thought about in twenty years takes the words of protest that are forming in my throat and shoves them back down somewhere deep inside. I'm not whining anymore.

Because of the name.

Adonna Moore.

"Oooh, we got Scoot's attention," Eric grins.

What is it about that name?

"Well, well," Erica says. "This is news to me. I didn't know you had a...thing for her."

"I didn't."

"Then how come you're looking so mooney?"

"I dunno." I grab the yearbook from Eric and study the picture. Adonna Moore. She was one of those girls in high school that you notice but don't notice. She was mildly pretty; what my mom would've called "attractive". She had that kind of tomboy thing going. She was jocky—I think she played basketball and softball—and if I remember she was very sure of herself. I had her in a few classes, might've even dissected a frog with her, and I always thought she was okay. Nice. Forgettably pretty.

Attractive.

But now, so many years later, something strikes me about her. It must be the wisdom of hindsight, the 20/20 view looking back. I realize she was special. I just didn't know it at the time.

I study the picture.

Long hair, brown expressive eyes, nice facial structure, strong shoulders, alert, intelligent....

Why the fuck didn't I pay any attention to this girl in high school? What was I thinking?

"Did she have a boyfriend?" I ask. "I don't remember."

Erica frowns, trying to remember. "She was a jock. That's all I recall about her."

"I don't think so," Eric says. When Eric concentrates it's really obvious, like some kind of head muscle is flexing. "Seems to me some guys on the team asked her out and she blew 'em off. They talked about her like she was a lesbo."

"Eric," Erica sighs. "You sound like such a cracker."

Eric shrugs. I doubt he knows what a cracker is.

"Great," I say. "One that might have potential and she's probably a leather dyke."

"So you find her and bring her back to the manly side."

"I don't think I'm the right guy for that," I say.

Erica watches me oddly. Like she suddenly doesn't trust me. "How come I didn't know about this?" she asks. It's as if she's my wife and I just confessed to boning the next door neighbor.

"I told you. Something just struck me when Eric said her name."

"What?"

"That she might've been special."

Erica yanks the yearbook from my hands, and the sudden grumble-shout of fighting children floats into the living room from the back of the house. "See what they're up to," Erica orders, and Eric meekly trots off to be Super-Daddy. Erica glares at the photo of Adonna Moore.

"Are you jealous?" I ask, laughing but incredulous.

"She's not that hot," Erica says, slamming the yearbook closed. "You could do better."

"You got a problem with her?" I ask, goading. This is turning fun.

"No!"

Eric comes back out carrying weepy, snotty-nosed Elishaba. Little Eli tags along, whining, "I didn't do anything!" Which, of course, means that he did. But seeing Eric carrying his weepy little cute-as-a-button daughter stabs me with a sharp pain of loss.

Crystal. My own daughter. Already rapidly becoming even more estranged from her dad. I'm sure Dr. Dwayne knows more computer stuff than me. He's probably playing some horrendously violent video game with her right now, blasting aliens they've named "Scooters" to smithereens.

I look at Erica. She's sitting with her arms folded, pouting. Strange. I'll never understand people—especially women. Even Erica, who I know better than anybody in the world, is capable of utterly baffling me. A few minutes ago she's all into this stupid woman hunt scheme, now she's seething with apparent jealousy because I acted mildly interested in somebody from twenty years ago. A potential lesbian I'll never meet.

I decide things couldn't get any weirder, and beg off to go be alone in the Airstream. Eric and Erica tend to their brood. Eric says goodnight.

Erica doesn't.

Weird.

The Airstream is pretty comfy; it's all I need, really. A little musty, and there's a few mouse turds around, but all in all it's an okay place to hang. Lots of closet space, nice little sink and toilet, comfy bed. Eric even hooked up an ancient black-and-white TV to the cable for me. What a guy. Always so thoughtful.

I flake out on the bed and channel surf. The images are tiny and grainy, but as always I stop surfing at the Discovery Channel and watch as a bunch of gonzo dinosaur scientists dig up bones. They're more like rock stars than science geeks, and I wonder if they're actors. Harrison Ford has had a big effect on these guys. I bet the old style sci-nerds are insanely envious of these studs with their earrings, tattoos and really hot graduate assistants. It's like an old Van Halen video.

But I soon lose interest; no matter how you edit it, watching people tweeze and toothbrush stuff out of sandstone gets boring.

I surf onward.

Until the cell phone rings.

I hesitate, but I decide it can't be anything bad, because what more bad news could I get? It's probably some telemarketing geek; maybe I'll have some fun with him. If it's for carpet cleaning I'll ask if they can get massive amounts of blood and brain matter out of hi-lo Berber.

"'lo?" I say suspiciously. Always good to sound a little crazy to a telemarketer.

"Daddy?" Crystal says, and my heart breaks.

"Hi honey!" I say. Tears immediately well in my eyes, and I realize how beat-up I am about this. I've been in denial.

"Guess what?" she says, sounding breathless and excited like she used to sound when she was little and I was still her hero.

"What?" I say, wiping a tear away and grinning hugely. Nothing like the sound of a tiny little voice saying, "Daddy" with love to cheer you up.

"Dr. Dwayne said I could go to computer camp this summer!"

If she had stabbed me in the heart with the sharpened heels of streetwalker Barbie I doubt it would've hurt as much. Because I can hear the triumphant snottiness in her voice; I'd told her last week we couldn't afford to send her to the computer camp she wanted to go to. Way too spendy.

"That's great," I say, icy. The warm Daddy thoughts are replaced with resentment and irritation.

I don't like this kid very much.

The phone slams down, and I'm about to click off, when Jane comes on. "You there, Scooter?"

"Yeah. Glad Dr. Dwayne can afford to do the right thing for Crystal."

"Yeah," Jane says without the slightest irony. "He's a good provider."

Jesus. A good provider?! She's talking like they've been married for twenty fucking years!

"You want something, Jane?" I ask. I am SO sorry I answered the phone. What was I thinking?

"I thought you should know, Dr. Dwayne and I spoke to the attorney today."

"Yes...."

"And we decided it would be best if you didn't have visitation rights with Crystal. It would just confuse her, and we want a stable home life for her with Dr. Dwayne."

"I—"

"You can fight it, of course," she says, "but do you really want to? Is it that important? Because I've never gotten the feeling that you care all that much about your daughter."

It's right now that I make a choice. I could rant and rave, scream and threaten, call her names, do the aggrieved spouse thing.

But I don't.

Because she's right. I don't care all that much. Maybe someday, maybe when Crystal is older and not so snotty, then we'll reestablish our relationship. But there isn't one now. And I'm not sure I want one.

So I click the phone off.

There's nothing more to say.

It's funny though; as I flip through the channels desperate for something to watch, something to take my mind off my life, tears roll down my cheeks and drip off the bottom of my jaw. I don't know the last time I cried this much. Maybe never.

After a while the tears slow, then stop. I'm rubbing snot pearls on my sleeve when the cell phone rings. I shouldn't answer it. If it's Jane with more fucking divorce demands I don't think I could take it, or if it's Crystal with triumphantly bratty "Guess what Dr. Daddy Dwayne's gonna let me do!" I *know* I can't take that.

But I have the feeling it isn't either one of them. So I answer.

Well, not answer, really. I click the phone on and say nothing.

And I'm greeted with nothing but the faintest hint of breathing. So I breathe back. It's like two obscene phone callers are on the same line.

I wait. Who is this? Not Jane. Jane doesn't let a minute, a second, keep her from giving her opinion. And it's not Crystal. Dr. Dwayne maybe? Feeling guilty that he stole my family, he's calling to apologize but can't find his voice?

I finally give in.

"Who is this?" I whisper.

"Are you sure about Adonna Moore, Scooter?" Erica whispers back. Her voice sounds strangely thick, like she's got a cold. But unless she caught one in the last hour I don't think that's it.

"Do you always call people and just breathe at them?" I ask. "It's creepy."

"Are you sure about Adonna Moore?" she asks again, stronger. I realize her voice is thick with...anger? Jealousy? Something weird I've never heard before.

"Erica," I say, trying to sound final. "I don't give a fuck about Adonna Moore, I don't give a fuck about anybody from high school or college or anywhere else. I'm not going on this goofy woman scavenger hunt. We were just talking, kidding around. My fucking life has crashed and burned, do you honestly think I can go do something this stupid a write a best seller out of it?!"

Erica doesn't usually piss me off, but right now I'm steaming. She's not being a supportive best friend. She's being a weirdo.

"If you go," she says, "you have to promise me something."

"I'm not going anywhere! I'm going to live in your Airstream trailer for the rest of my life!"

"If you find her, and if anything...happens between you—"

"Nothing's gonna happen!"

"I want you to know. I want you to realize that if I hadn't married Eric—"

"I don't want to hear this!"

"I want you to know that I've always regretted not...being with you. You know that, don't you?"

"Erica—"

"And if you want, I'll..."

"Don't say it. Don't say anything else. You and Eric are forever, Jesus, you've got a million kids, what are you saying?!" I *know* what she's saying, but I don't know what else to say.

"If you find her, what'll you do?"

I sigh. "I don't know, Er. I'm not gonna find her. I'm not gonna look for her. I'm not gonna look for anybody, I'm not gonna look for anything except a job and someplace to live."

"Are you sure about her?" she presses on. "There were lots of others."

"What's your problem with Adonna Moore?" I ask, intrigued by her weirdness about somebody from our distant past. "You have a fight with her or something?"

A long silence, then a tired sigh. A sniff. I imagine her in the den, cordless phone pressed hard to her face, her freckles angry red, eyes watery. I know exactly how she looks, the expression of her eyes, the tilt of her head, everything about her. I know Erica so much better than I ever knew Jane. I could be sitting in the same room with Jane, and if I closed my eyes I could forget what she looked like. Not Erica. She's such a part of me that I know her better than myself. At least I thought I did until this Adonna stuff started.

"Okay, then," she whispers. "Tomorrow we start."

"Start what?" I say.

"Tomorrow...." is all she says.

Chapter Three

The pounding on the Airstream echoes with a metallic *clank.* I try to open my eyes, but they're glued shut by sleep boogers, and anyway, why get up? No job, no wife, no life.

Might as well sleep the day away.

But that pounding won't let me.

As I come back into consciousness, I imagine the source of the sound. It's not really metallic, I decide, it's more of a thud against metal. If I didn't know I was in an Airstream trailer, I probably wouldn't even think there was a metal tinge to the sound.

But as I intellectually theorize the sound's source, it just keeps on getting louder and louder, more annoying and insistent and pretty soon I'm gonna have to tear my eyes open and make the sound stop, because no way am I going to be able to sleep.

"What?!" I grumble. Why won't the world just let me alone?

"Get up!" Erica's voice orders, muffled and softened by the Airstream's insulated walls. But not muffled enough to shave off the irritation. "It's after ten!"

"So?"

"So get up. We've got work to do!"

"I don't have to work. I got fired."

"GET UP!"

And I do, because she's pissed. She's in Mom mode, and I still respond to that tone of voice even though my own mom has been dead ten years. Once an obedient little boy, always an obedient little boy.

I stumble to the door and fling it open. Big mistake. The sun blinds my newly-peeled-open crusty eyes and it hurts like somebody's driven spikes into my head.

"Cute," Erica says. I peek through my fingers at her. She's dressed casual, cute as ever, with Eli and Elishaba at her side. "Don't mind Uncle Scooter," she tells the kids. "He didn't sleep well."

"He's wearing underwear," Eli giggles with mock horror, and I realize I'm standing in the Airstream's doorway with saggy boxers and nothing else. I look down. At least my dick's not hanging out. Wouldn't be a good thing for the little kids to see.

My mouth tastes gritty, like I ate sand for dinner, and as I blink my eyes into focus the pounding starts in my head. Like a hangover, but all I had was a few beers.

"Uh," is all I can think of to say.

"Get dressed," Erica orders. "We've got work to do. And I'll make you breakfast."

"Uh," I repeat.

After a shower and cup of coffee I'm starting to feel human. I don't know why I'm so lethargic this morning. It's like I've been drugged.

Erica mounds hot, steamy pancakes before me, along with a good load of greasy sausage links and plenty of coffee and orange juice. Ooohhh, baby, it tastes good. The chubby bulge that's beginning to ooze over my belt doesn't need it, but so what? Who am I trying to please? I'm single; if I want to blimp out I'll blimp out.

"Mmmgood," I say as maple syrup and melted butter dribbles down my chin. Erica knows how to make killer breakfasts—must be the secret to keeping all her rugrats happy.

"Uncle Scooter's messy!" Elishaba giggles, adorable and endearing. Too bad they have to grow up. In ten years she'll probably have pierced nipples, green hair, and be screaming at Eric and Erica to fuck off and let her have an abortion.

I shake my head. Negative thoughts. Not healthy. Not healthy at all. I concentrate on gorging myself.

Erica fusses with the kids and tidies way too busily. She's nervous and out of sorts. I'm not sure, but I think she still might be mad about the weird Adonna stuff. Who knows? The only thing I'm planning to do today is hit the unemployment office and get those checks coming in. And then maybe I'll lie out in the sun. I haven't had a good tan for a long time.

I finally finish the breakfast. My gut's so full it feels like it'll burst like in the *Alien* movies. "Good stuff, Er," I say. I feel almost good about the world at the moment. Nothing like a huge, stroke inducing breakfast to put you at peace.

"Glad you liked it," she says, but with sarcasm. What's the matter with her?

"Well," I say. "Guess I'll head out."

She pulls some sheets of paper out of a manila folder sitting on the counter. "Here."

"What're these?" I ask, expecting...well, I don't know what I was expecting.

"Directions," she says.

And as I look at the inkjet prints my stomach full of sausage and pancakes turns against me. "Erica...." I say.

"Elizabeth found the info in about a half hour on the computer. These kids are amazing in what they can dig up."

Maps. Precise directions. Phone number. Address. Email. Everything I could possibly need—

To contact Adonna Moore.

"I'm not going to do this."

"Sure you are. You want to, really. Inside. If you're honest."

Erica stands, arms folded, watching me. The kids scamper into the living room to destroy more toys.

"No, I'm not."

Erica comes over and sits next to me. She grabs my arm and lasers me with her eyes. I couldn't look away if I wanted to.

"Listen to me, Scooter. Do this. Do it for me."

"You're not making any fucking sense! You act all weird and jealous about this stupid deal, and then you want me to do it? What's wrong with you? You used to be normal."

"I think you should show up. No call, no letter, no email. Just show up. She's single, you know."

"Really?" I ask, more interested than I should be.

"Divorced. No kids."

"How do you know all this?"

She shrugs. "Elizabeth found it. Public records."

"How about her Visa Card number?"

"If you want," Erica grins her grin of old.

"I'm not doing this."

"Are the batteries in your laptop charged?"

"Erica...."

"You need to start writing. I think this morning...no, go back even further. Start when Jane dumped you."

"Erica...."

"You've got to start taking notes, at least. You won't remember all this good dialogue."

"What good dialogue?!"

"The clever stuff that I say. Make sure when you write about me you put in what good shape I'm in for having all the kids. And mention my hair."

I sigh. What else can I do? "And freckles," I add.

"You've always liked them, haven't you?"

I thumb through the sheets of paper, the World Wide Web history of Adonna Moore.

"There's no picture," I say. "I wonder what she looks like now?"

"Only one way to find out."

I set the papers down and look at Erica long and hard. "Why?" I ask. "Why do you want me to do this?"

"I want you to be happy, Scooter. I let you down a long time ago, I owe you now."

"You don't owe me anything, Er. As long as you stay my best bud."

"And I always will. But I want you to do this. I want you to find somebody, Adonna if it has to be, but I want you to be happy and I want you to be successful. That's why I want you to write about it. And make it funny, like you are."

"You overestimate my comic appeal."

"Everybody loves a loser."

"Maybe I should make that the title."

Erica cradles my hand in hers. "Please, Scoot. Find her and be happy."

My mouth opens. No words come out. I was going to tell Erica no, that I'm not going to go off and do this, that I'm not desperate, that I think it's harebrained and foolish and the whole notion is more sad than anything else....

But I don't say that. My mouth hangs open like I'm brain damaged, and Erica, in her eerie way, knows what's going on. Because she smiles that knowing Erica smile, that "I know you better than yourself" grin she throws at me, and I know that she knows that I now realize that for the hell of it and why the fuck not what else do I have to do anyway—

—I'm going to go find Adonna Moore.

"This is so...bitchin'" Eric says. He's grinning like a dork and I feel really sorry for him. First for using the word "bitchin'", and second for grinning like a dork. He's so excited I feel guilty that it's me and not him who's going.

Erica and some of the kids stand by the car. Erica grimly surveys the trunk I've loaded with my junk. "You got everything you need, Scooter? You sure?"

"Socks, underwear, rubbers—" and at the word "rubbers" little Eli chortles and runs around the front yard screaming "RUBBERS".

"He likes the word," Eric says, blushing as he chases the shrieking little kid. I'm amazed that Eric gets embarrassed so easily. Being born again makes you a pansy.

"Nice going, Scoot," Erica sighs tiredly.

"Where'd he learn the word?" I ask.

"From a storybook about a rainstorm. It's an old one and they call boots rubbers. What can I say? He thinks it's a funny word."

"Maybe you guys oughta pry open your wallets and buy the kids books that were published in the last century."

"RUBBERSRUBBERSRUBBERS!"

"Anyway," Erica says, ignoring the noise, "are you sure you've got what you need?"

"Yes, Mommy."

"The main things: cameras and laptop?"

"Yep." Erica not only wants me to write constantly about everything that happens, she wants lots o' pix for the book. Whatever. I've humored her so far. Who knows, if this deal turns out maybe I *will* take pictures. Naked ones if I get lucky with Adonna.

"Maps? Directions? Phone numbers?"

"Check, check, check. Commando Scooter is ready to begin the mission, sir."

"Shut up," Erica says, smiling.

I slam the trunk shut. Elishaba joins her father in chasing Eli around the yard, and pretty soon the entire litter of kids is running around, laughing, rolling, shouting, and Eric is covered with kids. It's kind of cute in a way, a happy family of religious rowdies. Erica watches her brood and smiles wistfully, like she loves it, loves them, but she's weary.

"This isn't so bad, Er," I say.

"I suppose," she says, turning back to me. "I love them so much."

"I know."

"Then how come I wish I was going with you? That you weren't off looking for Adonna Moore without me?"

I kiss her softly on the forehead. A few strays of her curly hair gently float on the breeze. "I'll call you."

"Email, too. I want to know every step of the way."

"It's probably not—"

She holds up her hand and stops my words. "Just go," she says. "Give it a shot."

And with a wave to Eric and the kids, I climb into the Camry and motor on down the street.

It's crazy, I decide again, I don't know what I'm thinking, why am I doing this? It's nuts, stupid, crazy....

But kinda fun.

And as I turn the corner it suddenly becomes like a movie, I imagine the throbbing backbeat of some cool music, the way the shot would be lit, how they'd cut away as I drive, to a long shot, the Camry on the road, Jimmy "Scooter" Biffman, on the QUEST!

And, on the DOWNBEAT—

We SLAM CUT to:

Chapter Four

LOSER: JIMMY "SCOOTER" BIFFMAN'S SEARCH FOR THE PERFECT WOMAN

The blood red sun hangs like a rotten peach over the bone-dry, distant mountains. It's sunrise in the Mojave desert and I'm driving along a lonely two lane asphalt strip, my mouth already dry, watching that bloody sunrise as it....

Fuck. I'm no writer. Jesus Christ. Purple prose, that's what it's called. "Blood red sun." God. I can't do this. I write fucking sports stories, interviews with zit-faced high school juniors who hit home runs and catch touchdown passes.

Not "blood red sunrises."

I can't do this.

The only part that's right is "loser."

I'm at a rest stop somewhere in the desert, sitting in the front seat of the sweltering Camry, tapping away on my laptop because I'm too afraid to go sit on the splintery picnic tables underneath some scraggly trees. There's a bunch of biker-looking guys hanging around, with lots of tattoos and equally terrifying-looking women. I went into the bathroom to pee, and as I leaned into the urinal, unable to perform because of the dreaded public restroom performance anxiety, I had time to study the graffiti scratched into the wall. Along with the usual "fucks" and "eat shits" there was one that really caught my eye: a swastika with the words "wite power" scratched beneath it. Great. The bozos who think they're the master race can't even spell one syllable words.

I gave up trying to pee when a couple of shaved-head muscle guys strolled in, and I figured I was lucky to get out alive—or at least unraped.

So now I'm trapped in the 110-degree Camry, jotting down my ravings, because Erica wants me to WRITE IT ALL DOWN! But the key's in the ignition, and I'm ready to fire it up and get the hell outa Dodge if anybody makes the least threatening move toward me. So far I'm completely ignored, but that could change.

So anyway, back to the...I hesitate to call it a book since I haven't really written anything yet. Okay. New idea. I'm not gonna try to be Norman Mailer, I'll just take notes. Like a diary. That'll be easier. Just write down what happens and leave out the gooey stuff about "blood red sunrises".

So.

Here we go.

TAP. TAP. TAP.

I don't have anything to say.

Maybe I should go back to blood red sunrises and bone-dry mountains.

"Hey man," a gravelly voice says, knocking me out of my writer's block and into the real world. I look up, and a few inches from my face is the face of a psychotic monster, the kind of face that, if you were dreaming, would have you lurching up in sweat-tangled sheets screaming, "PLEASE DON'T KILL ME!"

In the millisecond it's taken my eyes to see him and my brain to process the image, I know for sure I'm looking into the eyes of my killer. The last human I'll see on earth.

"Hey man," he repeats. I study his face. A spider web tattoo covers his neck and one cheek, and a tiny swastika held by a scowling eagle—with the words "white power" spelled correctly—is pulsing in that squishy soft spot at the base of his neck. My balls tingle at the thought of getting a tattoo there.

I'm such a weenie boy.

But it doesn't matter anymore, because spider-web-swastika-psycho-man is gonna kill me. I hope Crystal remembers me fondly, and I'm already feeling nostalgic for the meeting with Adonna Moore that I'll never have.

"You know where Fleenerville is, man? You got a map in that computer?"

"Fleenerville?" I croak. It comes out raspy and squeaky. I sound like a young girl.

"Yeah, man," he says. "I don't wanna fuckin' go the wrong way on the highway, man."

"Don't blame you," I say. I notice that he has one missing front tooth, and the other is capped with gold. He looks like a caricature, like one of those WWF clowns, except I know his body slams aren't fake.

And he's going to kill me.

Maybe I should just hand him the laptop. I wonder if that'll satisfy him? I try to picture my death; will I die with honor and dignity, or will I squeal and cry? Will it be a gunshot to the head? A stab wound to the throat? Or a garrote with nylon rope?

Whatever method he uses, I hope it's quick and relatively painless.

"You fucked up or something, man?" he asks. Here it comes. He's going to pretend to get mad at me, and that'll be his excuse. I've seen enough movies to know how this works. He'll taunt me with a DeNiro, "You talkin' to me!?" thing and then he'll strike.

"What?" I say.

The psycho guy frowns and for a moment looks human. "You dusted? Crank? Gotta be careful with that shit, man. I done time 'cause of it. It'll fuck you up forever, man."

"Okay."

"A map?" he asks.

I fumble around and find the sheets that Elizabeth made for me from the computer. I hold them up, but my hands are shaking so bad the psycho killer can't read them. He gently takes the sheets from me, studies them, and nods. "Glad I fuckin' asked. It's south. Woulda been bad news to go the wrong way." He hands the maps back to me and smiles. It's beginning to occur to me that maybe he isn't going to kill me. Or maybe he's just an exceptionally cruel killer who likes to toy with his victims before he does the deed.

"Anything else I can do for you?" I ask. My powers of speech are returning, and the sense that I might actually have a future on the planet has taken hold.

"No man. Gotta get to Fleenerville soon, though. My sister's havin' chemo, needs her baby brother."

"Oh," I say. Maybe he's not so bad. If you forget about the white supremacist stuff and the ultra-scary looks, he's just a concerned little brother. I'd think it was cute if I wasn't so run through the wringer with horror.

"Do me a favor, man," he says. "Stay off the road until you're straight. I been in some nasty-ass crashes while I was fucked up, man, I know. And go into rehab. Kick the shit and find the Lord. Worked for me, man." And with a friendly clap on the shoulder he strides off to his Harley hog, fires it up, and roars off down the road to his cancer-ridden sister.

I sit in the steamy Camry feeling like a dope. I *am* a dope.

But then I realize something important. My self-imagined brush with mortality and the scary-but-cool biker psycho have proven an important point:

This book is going to write itself.

The desert miles click off, one after another, ten after ten, hundred after hundred. Shit, this country's huge. How did the explorers figure this place out? I can't imagine plodding along out here, following my nose, wondering what's over the next scrubby mountain range. Killer Indians, more desert, monsters? *I'm* afraid and I'm in an air-conditioned Camry on a paved U.S. highway.

It's good I'm having these thoughts, though. They all go into the 'puter. Maybe if I can think of something witty or droll I can throw that in and please Erica.

I talked to her last night. It was an odd conversation. I had a hard time hearing her because the couple in the room next door were in the midst of screaming, throbbing, balls-to-the-walls sex. I'd never heard sex last so long and sound like so much fun. It made me sad to think I'd been married for all those years and never once had anything been so remotely enjoyable.

"What are they doing?" Erica asked as the fleshy thuds against the cardboard wall mixed in with squealy delight and muffled cries of, "Yes! More!!"

"What do you think, Er?" I replied. Dryly. Very dryly.

It was a trucker's motel in a nasty little mining town whose name I've already forgotten. I'd had an angioplasty special for dinner at the greasy spoon next door—everything was chicken fried, even the salad. The grubby patrons all looked like they were on parole, but I decided that maybe my white bread middle class paranoia was getting the best of me. I hustled out of there, though, when a couple of hard-drinking pot-bellied good old boys started watching me and snickering.

No need looking for trouble.

Boy, what a pussy. This trip will be good for me, toughen me up.

If I survive.

So anyway, back to Erica. "Are you getting lots of good stuff?" she asked, and I told her about the rest stop. She thought it was hilarious—Erica's always been amused by my stupidity—and I filled her in on the rest of the excitement, which was basically the mind-numbing drive and the sex next door.

"Make sure you write about how noisy they are," she said.

"Yes, dear."

"And don't leave anything out."

"You want me to go knock on the door and ask if I can take pictures?"

"Sure!"

"Shut up, you dork. I've already had enough brushes with death."

"Ooooh, yeah. Born-again biker. Lucky you survived."

We bantered for a while, but I was getting tired. I begged off with an "I gotta get some sleep," and then she said something odd.

"Scooter," she said, her voice suddenly serious. "Remember *The Quest.*"

"What?"

"*The Quest.* It's noble. You've got to hook up with her."

"Erica...."

"And if you don't, remember the alternative."

I didn't want to get into all that weirdness again, so I pretended I couldn't hear her, which was almost true because somebody next door was nearing their orgasm and things were getting really loud.

But now, as I drive through the desert, I think about what Erica said. It sounds to me, and maybe I'm being stupid again, that she's really serious about ditching Eric. No matter what, I decide, she won't come to me. I couldn't do that. Be a home wrecker. It would be sleazy and wrong and I don't know how people can do it.

But for the next hundred miles it's all I'm thinking about, and Adonna Moore quickly recedes into the back of my mind....

"May I speak to Adonna Moore, please?" I ask at the Forest Service office. Smokey the Bear glares down at me from a huge poster, frowning and wagging a finger/paw; *Only you can prevent forest fires.* The poster's unsettling. I've always thought that a bear wearing Levi overalls and a ranger hat is vaguely creepy.

A granola-momma in Forest Service greens is behind the counter, busily stacking pamphlets. She's got the leather skin of a serious outdoorsy type; probably well on her way to melanoma-hood.

"Adonna doesn't work here anymore. She hasn't worked here for a year," she says grinning with big buckteeth. She acts like she's delivered the best news in the world, and I should be gooey with joy. Why would I ask for Adonna Moore if I didn't want to find her?

I sigh and look up at the giant rough-hewn beam running down the length of the ceiling. The whole office is built from logs, massive logs. I'll bet enviros who stop by to visit are thoroughly pissed.

"A year," I say. Shit. Just as well. Stupid lame brain idea.

An eager-looking young guy with a beard and ponytail wanders out from a back office. He's dressed in the uniform too, and immediately strikes me as a dork. Something about the way he walks.

"You're looking for Adonna?" he asks.

"Yeah."

"She doesn't work here anymore. She hasn't for a year or so."

"I know." This guy has been in my life thirty seconds, and already I want to smack him. I know the type: always waving his hand at the teacher, "Call on me! Call on me!" and burrowing his nose deeply into the rectum of any authority figure. A true spazboy.

"Might have been longer than a year," Granola says. "Maybe a year and a half."

"No," Spazboy disagrees. "Thirteen months, max."

"Whatever," I say, disgusted. These two are geeks and I just want to get out of here and get back on the road to my life. Stupid ass idea. Why did I let Erica talk me into this?

I'm about to turn and leave this place forever when for some reason I'll never know I ask, "Do you know where Adonna is?"

"Well, sure," Spazboy says.

I resist the urge to rip out his throat. "Could you tell me where?"

And now he looks at me suspiciously, like I might be a crazed serial sex killer trying to hunt down and mutilate his former co-worker. Which is always possible, I suppose.

"How do you know Adonna?" he asks.

"We went to high school together. I want to look her up," I say.

"Oh," he grins. Spazboy apparently has decided I'm no threat. But he doesn't say anything, and Granola keeps busily piling up pamphlets.

"Are you planning on telling me where I might find her?" I ask through gritted teeth. I can see why the backwoods crazies hate the government if they have to deal with nimrods like these two. It's enough to make me want to stop paying taxes.

"She lives in Skull Peak."

"Where's that?" I ask. "I don't recall seeing a town by that name on my maps."

Granola and Spazboy exchange glances and snicker. "Well," Spazboy says, with a superior, "I'm more educated than you" smirk, "that's because it doesn't really exist anymore." And with that they both guffaw.

"Excuse me?" I say. If I only had a weapon....

"Skull Peak's a ghost town. Adonna's the caretaker ranger."

"How do I get there?"

Spazboy rummages around through a pile of papers and hands me a millionth-generation Xerox of squiggly lines and blurry names that apparently was once a map. "Just follow the directions," he says helpfully.

"How long will it take?" I ask.

"Oh, probably three or four hours. Depends on the road."

"Why?"

"Well, you know, how bad of shape it's in."

"Don't forget that huge thunderstorm last week," Granola says. "I think there might be some tough spots."

"The road's not so hot?" I ask.

"Skull Peak was a silver mining town," Spazboy explains. "Sometimes the minerals weren't in the most accessible places."

"Whatever," I say, just wanting to get the hell out of here. "Thanks."

As I'm going out the door I hear Spazboy saying something about "jeep" but I don't bother to stop and listen. I want to get back on the road and go find

Adonna.

It's weird. A few minutes ago, when I thought she was gone, I was ready to ditch the whole thing. But now that I know she's not far away, I'm really into it again.

Maybe it's the idea that she's an outdoorsy ranger living in a ghost town. I like the idea of a self-reliant woman, a wilderness babe in a uniform. I'll bet she hunts and fishes and can shoot a gun and uses the "F" word a lot.

This is going to be interesting.

As I follow the highway, it starts a gradual rise out of the desert. The scrubby desert brush gives way to scrubby pines, and as the Camry labors up a long grade, the air cools noticeably. Just as I reach the top of the grade, an enormous vista of snow-quilted granite peaks is before me. The miserable desert is immediately forgotten, replaced by craggy mountains and green, lush meadows. I smell moisture in the air now, and a stream rolls alongside the highway. Wow. A few miles, and what a change. I roll down the window and let the cool, pine-scented air wash over me. It's glorious.

I'm tooling along, communing with the alpine views, when I come to a huge sign pointing to the left: *Skull Peak—15 miles*. Sure glad they gave me the map; like I couldn't have found this on my own.

I pull off the highway onto a rutted gravel road. The Camry bounces along, but seems to be doing okay. Another gunshot-riddled sign says, *Four-wheel-drive recommended.* Maybe I should worry, but it does say recommended, not required, so how bad could the road be?

The road zigs and zags up the side of an ominously large hill. Further on, the giant peaks soar above, and I'm wondering how high up this ghost town is. I stop and study the map that Spazboy gave me. I run my finger along the outline of the road, and its alarmingly wavy curves. If it's that wavy on the map, I can only imagine what it's like further on. I decide maybe I better think about this before I continue.

I get out of the Camry and lean against the side, taking in the fresh air and gorgeous views. Wow. Spectacular. Makes me realize I should've vacationed in the mountains more. Jane insisted that our vacations be family-oriented, which meant *her* family, which meant long, dull, hot summer get-togethers with her parents and siblings and cousins and lots of other people I neither knew nor cared about. I used to spend a lot of time drinking beer with another outlaw named Dave. I don't know what Dave did; he was married to one of Jane's cousins, and by the time I got around to asking him about his line of work I'd usually had so many beers that even if he did tell me I could never remember. Or maybe he didn't tell me.

Or maybe I just didn't care.

Should've come to the mountains.

I sit on a fallen log and breathe in the magical air. The sky is blue, so blue. Little clouds puff to life up at the mountaintops, expanding from nothing into fluffy balls in seconds, only to be shredded back into nothing by the winds. A blue jay squawks at me as he passes by, and a fat thing that looks like a glandular gopher pops its head up from behind a rock and chirps at me. It takes me a minute to figure out that it's probably a marmot. I've never seen a marmot before, or clouds being born.

What a fucking sheltered life I've led. I've missed out on so much. And this is what Adonna Moore gets to experience every day of her life.

I've got to get to Adonna Moore. I know it's probably not going to happen—I mean, what are the odds of somebody from the past showing up and starting a relationship?—but I want to try. Erica's right.

It's all about *The Quest.*

I hop back in the Camry and bounce on up the road.

After some bone-rattling bottoming outs from going too fast, I finally learn that if I'm gonna make it to Skull Peak I'm gonna have to crawl. It'll take forever.

After a half-hour I get to the top of the zig-zaggiest part and see that the hill I've been climbing is puny compared to what's ahead. The road leads through crumbly granite scree, past fallen trees and on up into a valley between two huge peaks. I don't know how far Skull Peak is, but it must be a long ways off because I can see for miles and there's no sign of anything other than the winding path of the road.

I glance nervously at my gas gauge. Half a tank. Should be enough to get me there, and that's all that matters. Because who knows, maybe I won't be leaving all that soon.

"Fuckin' A," I murmur to myself. What if I stay at Skull Peak the ghost town with Ranger Adonna? What would prissy Jane and Dr. Dwayne the periodontist have to say about that?

And it's that righteous vengeance, the get-even we all want when somebody's butt-fucked us, that makes me kick the accelerator and spin a brodie in the gravel and go off to meet my destiny.

The Quest, baby!

When the Camry high centers a boulder and I blow the oil pan into shreds of slippery steel, *The Quest* suddenly seems a tad bogus.

I suppose it was stupid to be singing *Rebel Yell* at the top of my lungs and speeding along a miserable road in a Camry, but I couldn't help it. I was...juiced. Adonna. The mountains. Ghost town. Ranger Adonna. Scooter Biffman, every bit as macho as fucking Lewis and Clark, on an adventure, *The Quest*!

Until I tore the oil pan off and watched my dear, sweet Camry's vital fluids drain into a glistening chocolate syrup puddle on the impossibly rough road.

Four-wheel-drive recommended. Shit. Ten-wheel-drive would be more like it. Must've been what Spazboy was yelling about "Jeep" when I left the ranger station.

Shit.

It's 1:37 according to the Camry's clock. I should've had lunch before I headed up here. I rummage around in the back seat and find a half-eaten bag of Doritos I bought back at a mini-mart in the nasty mining town with the rambunctious sex neighbors, and there's a warm bottle of Evian.

And that's all I've got. Another chubby marmot squeaks at me. I wonder how hard it would be to catch one of those things if I needed to survive? It wrinkles its nose at me, as if it understands what I'm thinking, and vanishes into a rocky crevasse.

Who am I kidding? I won't survive a day out here. I'm a suburbia guy who can't live without ATMs and mini-mart Slurpees and Slim Jims and giant-sized Snickers bars.

I figure I've gone about ten miles from the main road, so all I've gotta do is hoof the last five to Skull Peak and then all will be well. Adonna probably shoots her own game for dinner. I've never had venison, but I'm willing to try...especially to be sociable and all. Gotta go native if I have a chance with Adonna.

So I pack up my 'puter and some clothes into a tiny backpack, lock the Camry—although I'm not sure why. It's not like anybody can steal it, and there's nothing of value inside other than the rest of my clothes, but those old city habits die hard and walking away from a car without locking it is unthinkable. Who knows, rowdy teenagers joyriding to the ghost town might wander by.

With one final, sad look at my loyal Camry, I start walking.

And after about twenty steps I have to stop and rest.

My heart's pounding, my legs feel shaky and gimpy like I've got some wasting neuromuscular disease. It's the altitude, and with the horrible realization the road only goes up from here, I know I'm in deep shit. Five miles might as well be fifty if I can only cover a little bit at a time before I have to stop and wheeze like a four-pack-a-day smoker.

But what choice do I have? None, zilch, nada. So off I plod.

And once I realize the need to pace myself, it isn't so bad.

I feel like those poor kids running wind sprints during two-a-days in August; I used to sit in the stands and bullshit with the coaches while their teams sprinted and puked and practically died. At the time I hardly noticed. I was Mr. Badass local sports reporter, they were just high school kids, no big deal. Now that I'm gasping and perilously close to blowing chow myself, I have new admiration for them.

I should've been more sympathetic.

But I decide I'll probably survive. Even though I feel like I'm getting about a tenth of the oxygen I need, I have faith in my underlying manly strength. Manly. Man-like. I've never used any permutation of "Manly" thinking about myself before, but why not start now? It's a major life change I'm going through, so it's time to start thinking differently about myself.

I plod along the road. I'm actually starting to feel pretty good about this. I'll walk into Skull Peak, dusty and sweaty and...*manly*...and boy, will I ever make a good impression on Adonna. This might be a real blessing in disguise, I mean, how pussyboy to come driving up in a Camry. It's so much more majestic to walk into a ghost town, gritty and tough, and say, "My rig broke down miles back, had to walk into town." It's the kind of thing you saw with a slow drawl. A manly drawl. I can picture Clint Eastwood or John Wayne saying it. Scooter Biffman, Western Hero.

The pleasant fantasy works its way onward, with Adonna impressed, inviting me into her place—I imagine her staying in the old sheriff's office, maybe a cot in the back—and venison cooked over an open fire outside, then lively conversation and reminiscences and then....

A bone-jangling THUNDERCRACK! blasts me back into the present, before the fantasy can get interesting. I look above, just in time to get splatted on the forehead with the largest raindrop I've ever felt. It's like a birdshit from a low-flying elephant, and I wonder how the black thunderheads could've formed so quickly. Another blast of thunder, and then the lightning starts.

Oh shit.

Lightning scares me.

The sky rips open with slashing, jagged flashes, crack-booms that hurt my eardrums, and cascades of water. I run along the road, my hands uselessly over my head—like my two pink little paws could protect me from anything—and I've never been so frightened.

I stumble and crash to the road, the rough rocks gouging my knees, scramble to my feet, and run on—

But the storm's getting worse, I smell the faintly chemical odor of ozone, and I realize that lightning is striking nearby, I zag off the road and into a thicket of pines, maybe I'll be safe until the storm passes, these mountain storms don't last long, do they?

And that's when I smell the ozone again. Weird, reminds me of an odor from the past, but I don't know what, but then, my hair tingles and I look down at my arm and all the hair is standing straight up like needles, and I feel the hair on my head standing up, and oh SHIT!, I've watched enough Discovery Channel to know that I'm about to get hit by lightning, and for some reason I don't think of saving myself, only the laptop, because if it gets fried Erica will never forgive me, so I pull off the backpack and throw it as far as I can, and as I watch it sail into the rainy sky the ozone smell is overwhelming and my hair dances and then a hammerblow hits and everything goes black....

Squeak!

I try to open my eyes, but it feels like they've been super-glued shut. Or maybe the eyelid muscles don't work anymore. Great, I'm a total body-plegic, I'll spend the rest of my days being fed through a stomach tube and *hissgasping* with a machine pumping my lungs through a hole bored into my throat.

Or maybe, must maybe, I'm dead! I mean, I don't really feel alive, and I can't move anything, not even my eyelids. But I don't know, I have enough sensation of living to think that maybe I'm not set to howdy-doo with Jesus just yet.

Squeak!

What is that sound? As I wonder, I suddenly feel my face. I can tell I have a face, it tingles and the muscles twitch. And now, just as suddenly, I can open my mouth. My tongue is huge and dry, and I lick my lips—they feel enormous. I try my eyelids again, and this time they reluctantly quiver open.

I'm looking into clear blue sky.

No storm clouds, so that's a good sign. And no St. Peter—or Satan—so I'm still among the living. But there's that damn squeak next to my ear and it's driving me nuts. I turn my head to see what it is. Big mistake, because a flaring, slashing pain hammers inside my skull, it feels like my head's gonna explode like an overripe melon, I slam my eyes shut and this time I wish I was dead....

And in a few minutes the searing pain passes. The squeaking continues, so I cautiously open my eyes and try to focus. Grey rock, the trees I dived into to escape the lightning...and a marmot. A big, fat, bucktoothed gooball sits a few feet away, nose twitching, squeaking and staring at me with dumb brown eyes.

I'm in sort of a vulnerable state right now, so I hope these things aren't carnivores. I doubt I could fight him off if he decided to start nibbling on my appendages.

"Get outa here!" I hiss, raspy-voiced and sore-throated. He squeaks, wrinkles his nose, and vanishes into the rocks.

I take a deep breath and carefully take a body inventory. I wiggle my toes, my fingers, tense my arms and legs. Everything seems to work.

I slowly sit up. The head-pounding is bad, but bearable. The sun is behind the peaks, and the air is noticeably cooler than before the storm. I don't know how much daylight is left, but I suspect not a whole lot. I stand on wobbly legs, and that's when I notice that the heel of my left Nike is missing...not missing, actually. Melted.

I scratch my left shoulder. There's a hole in the shirt, and burn marks track along my left side. My belt buckle is a molten mass, and the skin underneath burned nasty red and black. It only throbs a little, but I bet give it some time and it'll hurt like a son-of-a-bitch. I must've gotten hit on my left shoulder and it traveled down my left side and out through my shoe.

Fucking amazing.

I wonder if this means I'll have special powers now, like John Travolta in that stupid movie? Except it turned out he had a brain tumor and he croaked anyway. But shit, to survive a lightning strike, that's big time. I mean, do you get any luckier? Not that being hit is lucky, that's unlucky, but living to tell about it, man, I wish I could buy a lottery ticket right now. Is Adonna ever gonna be impressed! And wait until Erica hears about this...best seller, no matter what.

The laptop. Where did it end up? I hunt around the rocks and finally find the backpack wedged between a couple of big jagged boulders. Fresh marmot turds adorn it. Must've been that squeaky little shit who was bugging me when

I woke up. Or maybe he was the *reason* I woke up! Maybe it was one of those weird Rover-dialing-911 kind of deals, where a supposedly dumb animal shows superhuman intelligence to save a person's ass! But as I think about it, the squeaky marmot didn't do anything other than squeak and take a dump on my backpack, so it's probably best not to give him too much credit.

I open the pack and flip open the laptop. It fires right up. Good old Toshiba. I'll have to tell them what happened, maybe they'll use me in an ad touting Toshiba toughness.

Always thinking.

My brain's working faster than usual. Must be the electricity. I still feel weird, strangely euphoric and tingly, but it's not unpleasant. Nothing hurts anymore, my head's fine, the ugly burn on my gut is painless, everything's okey-dokey. Am I in shock? I don't think so, because it's not like I'm in any distress. Deep denial, maybe. I wonder if there's excess electricity zapping around inside me, will it finally get to be too much and fry my heart like microwave popcorn?

Nah. If I survived the original blast, there's no way I'm gonna die now. I'm fucking invincible, and this is truly meant to be. I've gotten divine proof that *The Quest* is the real deal.

Nighttime.

Owls hoot. Coyotes chatter. Things skitter in the darkness just beyond the road.

Are there bears out here?

The invincibility is starting to wear off. I've been trudging for a couple of hours, and it seems like I oughta be getting close to Skull Peak, but there's still no sign other than the ribbon of the road leading into the mountains.

I've decided that I was in shock, which must've loaded my system with natural painkillers—endorphins?—because now every muscle fiber in my body aches, the oozy burn on my gut behind the melted buckle shrieks stabby agony with every step, my head throbs, and I basically feel like shit.

Like a guy who got hit by lightning.

If I ever get to fucking Skull Peak, maybe I'll get Adonna to run me to the nearest hospital. A guy who was hit by lightning probably oughta be checked out by a doctor. Who knows what lurking shit inside is waiting to get me. Probably activated tumors, stretched arteries to the breaking point, I'll have strokes and embolisms and god knows what else.

So much for invincible.

But I stumble on through the mountain night. I'm getting hungry, but not thirsty—I crossed a creek a while back and tanked up on good, fresh mountain water. I was so thirsty it didn't occur to me until afterwards that the stream was probably teeming with bacteria, but it doesn't matter. I needed the water.

A quarter moon rises over the peaks, and even its dim light is enough to bathe the bright granite and patchy snow in a bluish light. If I wasn't so beat up and scared it would be beautiful. But right now I just want to find the fucking town and get...safe again.

Coyotes shatter the silence with spooky chatters, like a bunch of hyenas, and I break into a trot. I know they can't hurt me, unless they work as a pack and bring me down and tear me to shreds and oh, fuck, what a terrible way to die, I fucking survived a lightning strike but I'm gonna be eaten by a bunch of overgrown mutts who don't play by the rules, and—

Okay, stop it. Jesus, be a man. No wonder I never played sports in high school; too much of a girly-boy. It's not like I'm lost in the wilderness, I'm on a gravel road leading to a ghost town and a backcountry-savvy ranger who'll rescue me and I'll be okay even though I got zapped by lightning—how many people survive that?—and everything'll be okay, I know it, if only those goddamn coyotes would SHUT THE FUCK UP 'CAUSE THEY'RE SCARING THE CRAP OUTA ME!

And that's when I hear it.

Music.

I stop moving, but my hyperventilating gasps mask the sound, it's distant and soft. I stand for a few minutes, my breathing slows, the coyotes shut up, and then I know what I hear.

A guitar. Slow strumming. No vocal that I can hear, just a soothing tune, maybe folk, country, I dunno, but it's live, which means I'm getting near a human being, which means I can be safe from the scary night....

So I start running. The backpack bounces on my back, the laptop gouging me, but I don't care, I need to be safe, and the sore muscles and achy bones and oozing sore and lightning shocked body don't matter, because I'm nearing another person, probably Adonna, and now I'm almost delirious, I'm almost safe, run to the top of a rise, and before me—

Lies Skull Peak.

I stop running.

I can't move.

It sits in a small valley, surrounded by soaring peaks, and in the dim moonlight the ramshackle buildings look very spooky, the name ghost town fits too well, the only light is from the sky and reflection of snow-capped peaks and unnaturally glowing granite, it's weird, it's night but light out, I'm not sure except that maybe because the air is so clear and I'm so high up that starlight actually illuminates, but I can see Skull Peak clearly and now I'm not so sure—

It looks like a place where ghosts might really live.

Okay. Enough. I'm out of my mind right now, probably from the lightning, but I've got to get over the hysteria, maybe it's altitude-induced, whatever,

I start walking down the steep grade into town.

The guitar strumming is all around me, it echoes off the mountainsides and comes from all directions, surround-sound, digital DTS, clear and loud and I have no idea where it's coming from.

I enter the main street; old hitching posts like from John Wayne movies sag anciently in front of equally sagging buildings, waiting for ghost horses to tie up. I wander past broken windows and gaping doors, shrunken boards slowly sloughing off the sides of buildings with faded signs reading "Mercantile" and "Horseshoes" and "Saloon".

Oh fuck, this place gives me the willies.

The guitar strumming, soothing any other time, only adds to the eerieness, and I slowly move through the streets, past weathered gray boarding houses and saloons and even a church with a graveyard next door, and the crooked headstones—mostly wooden and split—grin like broken teeth at my fear.

This town is surprisingly large, and surprisingly confusing. I'm back on the main street before I realize it, and still I haven't figured out where the music's coming from and where Adonna is.

I could wander aimlessly, peeking into black doorways and ancient windows, but that would be stupid. It's time to take decisive action.

So I scream, "ADONNA MOORE!" as loud as my weary lungs will allow, and the booming echo pierces the night and sounds like it's bouncing through the mountain peaks for a thousand miles.

The guitar music abruptly stops.

"ADONNA? WHERE ARE YOU?"

No response. I realize it probably sounds pretty creepy to her, for some screaming maniac to be bellowing her name when she expected to be alone with her guitar and the ghosts of Skull Peak. I feel kind of bad all of a sudden, so I decide maybe I'd better clue her in on what's going on.

"IT'S ME, JIMMY BIFFMAN, FROM HIGH SCHOOL. I GOT HIT BY LIGHTNING." I wait for her reply, but nothing. Why doesn't she answer? I've cleared up the confusion, she must remember me, and she must've seen the storm that blew through here, why the games? I'm being honest, told her who I was and what happened to me.

And then it hits me. It probably did sound a little odd. *It's Jimmy Biffman from high school and I got hit by lightning.* Jesus, what an idiot. This isn't the entrance I wanted to make.

"LISTEN, ADONNA, I KNOW THIS SOUNDS WEIRD, I CAME TO VISIT, MY CAMRY BROKE DOWN, AND THEN I GOT HIT BY LIGHTNING, BUT I THINK I'M OKAY. ARE YOU HEARING ME?"

Nothing.

Shit. What the hell am I gonna do now? Maybe Adonna isn't really here, maybe she left or those knuckleheads at the ranger station didn't know what's going on, maybe somebody else is here, maybe Adonna is here but can't answer, maybe SOMEBODY MURDERED HER! My brain's buzzing with every idiotic possibility there is from aliens to Indian ghosts when the crunch of boots on dirt sounds behind me.

I spin, expecting ghouls or zombies or meth-head biker murderers or John Wayne's ghost or—

"Jimmy Biffman?" the silhouette asks. It's not a ghoul or a monster. It's a woman, and in the dim light I can't make out her face, but she has a soft, kind voice, her body is thin, she's wearing some kind of ranger hat, and as I try to focus I can see she's wearing a T-shirt and jeans and boots, and long hair cascades beneath the ranger hat, and I wish I could get a good look at her face—

"Adonna?" I ask breathlessly.

"Jimmy Biffman," she says, and I can tell she's saying it with a smile. "You were a band fag, weren't you?"

Okay, not the way I want to be remembered, but who can blame her? I *was* a band fag.

"Well, not anymore. I'm a sports reporter." I don't go into detail about my new circumstances. That can come later.

"What brings you to Skull Peak?" she asks. There's a smile in her voice. I wish I could see her face. From what I can see of her, the years have been kind. Not that it matters, because it's not like I'm Mel Gibson or anything and I have any reason to be uppity, but at least she's not huge.

"Actually," I say, suddenly wishing I'd rehearsed this part. I realize I don't have a clear idea of something to say that doesn't sound scary or weird. "I...." I stammer and I'm stumped. How do I explain to her what I'm doing?

"Are you all right?" she asks, taking a step closer.

"Well, the lightning...."

"You got hit? Really? Or was it just nearby?"

"There's a hole in my shoe and burn marks all over me. Direct hit, I'd say."

"Oh," she says, and the concern in her voice melts me. All those years with Jane and never once did she sound that concerned about me. Of course, I'd never just been hit by lightning, either.

"I think I'm all right, though," I say manfully. I try to be Harrison Ford-like, stoic and strong, like I've got a titanium scrotum.

"Let's get you inside," she says, and she comes closer and puts an arm around my shoulder. "I'm an EMT, I'll check you out, if you need it, I can run you down to the clinic in my rig."

It's weird, as she gets close to me, there seems to be a dark shadow on one side of her face. But the light is so dim, and with her hat and all that hair I can't really see her other than the whites of her eyes and her teeth as she talks, and as we walk I smell the clean freshness of her hair, healthy and outdoorsy, oh yeah, this is what I'm looking for in a woman, nice, caring, smells good....

"...so how did you find me? And why?" she's asking. I pull myself from my hair-smelling fantasies back into the now. I'm woozy and light-headed, and I'm not sure if it's from lightning and fatigue or excitement that I've finally hooked up with her.

"Remember Erica?" I ask.

"Vaguely. You were always hanging around with her. Didn't she marry that football lunkhead right outa high school?"

"Yeah. Eric."

"That's right," she laughs. "He was in my English class. Great looking, but with the IQ of a toilet seat."

"That's Eric," I say, wanting to defend him, but knowing she's basically right. She's smart and sassy.

I like that.

A lot.

"Well," I say, trying hard to come up with a lie that's acceptable—I'll tell her the truth later, when we've gotten to know each other better—"they have a slew of kids, and we were messing around one night, talking about high school, and one of their little nerd kids got onto the web and we looked up people from high school. You were one of them."

"Really?" she says. "Why would you guys be curious about me?"

"Oh, you know. Old times and all."

"But we hardly knew each other."

"You always struck me...as interesting."

"Oh," she says, and if I'm not mistaken I think she's flattered. "We're almost there. You holding up okay?"

"My knees are getting to be like Jell-O," I say, and that's the truth. I'm getting weaker and weaker and it's a little scary.

She leads me down an alley past dark back doors leading into hulking buildings. "It's kinda creepy around here," I say.

"You get used to it. Where we're walking right now is the back entrance to Skull Peak's biggest bordello. A hundred and twenty years ago, this alley would've been filled with drunk miners getting tossed out after they'd had their pleasure."

Had their pleasure. What a nice euphemism for fucking. I like Adonna's style; she's got class.

I find myself depending on her shoulder more and more now, and it's not because she's nice and friendly, it's because I'm getting close to passing out. Shit, I feel so weird suddenly, my head's buzzing with electric flies and my muscles twitch with minds of their own.

"Almost there," Adonna whispers into my ear.

She leads me past the ghost town streets, to a small prefab cabin tucked behind a fallen-down church.

"You don't get to live in one of the original buildings?"

"Nope. It's a living museum. Anyway, that'd be way too creepy, even for me."

A thundercrack splits the night. "Jesus!" I jump, pulling away from Adonna. No more fucking lightning, thank you.

"It's okay. Just another little storm blowing through. You'll be safe."

She gently takes my arm and pulls me toward the little cabin. It *does* look safe and inviting. We reach the door just as big raindrops splat and white-blue lightning flashes illuminate the night. I can't believe how quickly these storms come out of nowhere up here.

Just as we get to the cabin door, another huge lightning flash splits the night, and I see Adonna's face for the first time—

—And as I scream and my knees buckle and I collapse to the ground, I know I'm in a fucking nightmare, maybe the lightning killed me after all and this is some weird-ass joke that God's playing before he throws my ass into hell—

Because the last thing I remember before I plunge into the inky night of sleep or nightmares or death, the last image that sears itself forever into my brain—

—Is Adonna Moore's face—

She's not human, she's a fucking ghoul, grinning crookedly with a shredded leathery monster face from hell.

My screams fade away as the horror shuts off my brain and everything's black and silent.

Chapter Five

I've never been sure how to act around people who are fucked up.

Okay, that's harsh, but you know what I mean. When you go into Wal-Mart and the guy in the wheelchair smiley-faces you and small-talks about the weather, or the retarded kid across the street wants to discuss the color of the sky, or the old guy dragging an oxygen bottle with the tubes leading into his nose asks where the nearest 7-11 is—I never know what to say, how to act. I always try so hard not to notice that there's something between us that's different I end up uncomfortably tongue-tied, and the poor person who's just going about their everyday life gets mad or hurt that an insensitive goof like me can't just chill. It's a real character flaw, and it makes me small. I know it, I always have. And I've always felt guilty.

It's just that I don't seem to be able to do anything about it.

So that's why I'm in the quandary I'm in right now.

It's morning, I think the morning after Adonna rescued me, but I'm not sure. I could've been sleeping a week for all I know.

I feel unusually clear this morning. Last night's buzzy, lightning-induced freakishness has subsided, and I'm refreshed and rejuvenated. No more "I'M GONNA DIE!" thoughts trouble me, and I'm pretty sure that I am indeed still alive and kicking.

It's just that I'm not sure what to do next.

Right now I'm tucked in a slippery nylon mummy bag on a cot in the tiny cabin's main room. The only room. Adonna apparently uses the room for every part of her life—cooking, sleeping, hanging out. Luckily, I've noticed, there seems to be an outhouse, so at least when I finally get up I'll be spared the indignity of stinking up her pad.

But I'm not all that sure I want to get up.

Ever.

Because it all goes back to that problem I have, the one with fucked up people.

Because Adonna Moore is fucked up. Bad.

Now don't judge me on this. "Fucked up" is harsh, I know. She seems like a perfectly lovely person, and somebody who, in another situation, would be pursuable. It's just that with her...problem, well, I can't possibly—

God, listen to me. What a dick. I'm a miserable piece of human sewage, one without any redeeming qualities. No wonder Jane shit-canned me. She's no jewel, but at least she's honest. I'm a fucking scumbag, a liar, a...weakling.

Because right now, at this instant, as Adonna sits at a tiny table eating a bowl of cereal and reading an old magazine, when I should be rising-and-shining and thanking her profusely for her care and concern, I'm pretending to be asleep, stealing glances with one eye through a gap in the mummy bag's head that I've got pulled up over my own miserable, empty, rotten head.

Utter dirtbag.

She's clueless, of course. I purposely breathe slowly and evenly, pretending to be deep in dreamland. She occasionally glances my way, but so far I've been able to see it coming and slam my eyelid shut before she can make me. But I can't do it forever; unless I want to play possum, or pretend to die, or sneak out when she goes out, I'm gonna have to face this.

And I really don't want to.

I watch her as she eats. Her movements are delicate, feminine, yet there's nothing weak or wimpy about her. She's strong, suntanned and healthy—the kind of woman you'd expect to be a backcountry ranger in a ramshackle ghost town. Her body, from what I can tell, is nice; tight and slim. But it's her face, when I look at her face—

Because she's only got part of one. Like the old Mel Gibson movie, where he's the recluse who everybody thinks is a child molester, or whatever it was. I never saw it, just read the reviews. But Adonna Moore is the woman without a face. Or half a face, actually.

One side is stretched tight, with leathery crevasses and mottled discoloration. It's like she only has about two thirds of the skin she needs to cover the bone. Her lip is pulled hideously upward on one side, exposing her teeth in a perpetual snarl. Her eyelid is droopy and scabby, the skin scorched and unhealthy looking. It's weird, because if I concentrate at looking at the untouched side of her face, she's the same pretty kid I remember from high school. But the other side, jeez....

As I study the damage, I wonder how it happened. A burn of some kind, maybe, or a horrible accident that launched her face through something, glass, I dunno. I feel truly sad for her; it must be hell to have to go through life with a disfigurement like that, putting up with dicks like me who stare or studiously ignore or otherwise treat her differently.

I hate myself. I wish I could not notice it, I wish I could....

It doesn't matter what I wish. What I wish is that I'd never come here on this fool's errand, that I'd ignored Erica's crackpot idea, that I'd moved somewhere and started over after divorce and job loss, that I'd done what every other normal person does after life deals them some shitty cards.

But no. I go running after a dumbshit dream that under any circumstances never made one bit of sense.

Shit.

I decide it's time to get it over with. Get up, make some small talk with Adonna Moore, try gracefully to get this over with, and get the hell back to the world. I make a mental note to cut Erica out of my life while I'm at it. She's my all-time best buddy, but I think she's trouble for me now. Between her ideas and her weirdness about Eric and marriage, it's time for me to edit her out of my life. Her problems are her problems; I'm not going to be part of them.

I open my eyes and pull back the mummy bag. When Adonna looks over and smiles—at least with the one side of her mouth that works—my heart, well, it hurts. Because that smile, with its warmth and inner beauty, it almost erases the *Phantom of the Opera* side of her face, the scary look at something horrible.

Almost.

"Hey," she says, smiling and unselfconscious as if half her face isn't missing. "I was beginning to think I should check you for a heartbeat. Feeling okay?"

I sigh. Not because I feel bad, physically I feel great. It's just so...sad. "Yeah," I say, trying to avoid looking at her. "Little wobbly, maybe, but okay."

"Not surprised," Adonna says. "Last night after you passed out I called down to the hospital and talked to the ER doc. With the huge storm and all I couldn't get you down there, but I checked you over real good, and she said that unless other symptoms turned up you'd be one of the lucky ones."

"What kind of symptoms?" I ask, immediately alarmed. I feel good, but you never know. It's always good to be a little paranoid after you've been struck by lightning.

"Dizziness. Unconsciousness. Death. That's a big symptom. Death." And on the word "death", Adonna launches into laughter and I can't help but laugh along with her. Gee, she sure seems cool. Even better than I remembered from high school.

"Am I dead?" I ask. "Because I sure am hungry. And you don't crave Cap'n Crunch when you're dead, do you?"

I force myself to look into her eyes. If I only look at her eyes, it's okay. The one eye is a little creepy, but nothing serious. But I can't stop from looking lower, to that skeletal grin, the parchment skin, and I can't...make myself keep looking.

God, what a prick.

But if Adonna notices she doesn't let on. She tells me about the hikers she's heard of being killed instantly by lightning and freakish stories about people who did everything right, everything by the outdoorsman's book, who still got nuked.

"A guy in a car even got killed once," she continues, with that pleased note in her voice that people have when they're telling awful stories about somebody else's misfortune. People who talk about *her* probably sound the same way. "You know, the tires are supposed to insulate you, so that the lightning won't hit. But not this guy. He'd been doing some extreme biking up on a logging road, saw the storm, rode like crazy back to his old Subaru, climbed in, and got fried. Absolutely blasted. I was on the rescue team who found him; he looked like he'd been blow-torched. That's why I didn't believe you at first when you said you'd been hit."

The horror stories are making me queasy. But I've got to pee something fierce—that's a good sign, isn't it?—so I slither out of the mummy bag and stand on surprisingly strong legs. The shaky weakness of last night is gone.

And it's now that I realize so are my clothes. I'm standing buck naked in front of Adonna and her bowl of cereal, my pathetic little dick dangly sadly, like it's been neglected far too long and realizes it'll probably never be called to action again.

"'Scuse me," I mumble, pulling the mummy bag in front of me.

"Saw it all last night. Gave you a backwoods physical. I figured you were gonna survive when you popped a little chubby while I was feeling your ribs for fractures."

Well now. I should be embarrassed and humiliated, but Adonna's so offhand about everything I can't really be upset. It'd be tough to be embarrassed around her, I decide. She seems very cool.

I pull on my gamy briefs and scorched pants. The Levi's smell like they've been barbecued. "Be right back," I mumble, and Adonna nods and crunches her cereal. I catch a glimpse of milk leaking out of the damaged side of her mouth as she chews. She brushes the white droplets away with annoyance, as if they're mosquitoes or something equally trivial, and as much as I try I can't keep my stomach from somersaulting.

Maybe I'm just weak from all the excitement, but I don't think so. It's just so...creepy.

I stumble outside and immediately rip open a gash on the bottom of my foot when I step onto a razor-sharp rock. As I swear and bleed my way into the outhouse, I realize that even though the last twenty-four hours have been...unusual, I'm in a bad place. Nothing remotely interesting is going to happen here, the whole "Scooter's search for a woman" thing is dead in the water—not that it ever really had any life—and I'm nowhere. As soon as I get out of here, it's time for a major reality check, it's time to do something worthwhile, something real.

Shit.

I pee endlessly into the gaping pit toilet, holding my breath against the fumes welling up from below. My foot already throbs. I'm gonna have to get Adonna to dress it for me, for all I know I'll need stitches. This just keeps getting better and better.

And somehow, the worst thing, is that I'm gonna have to hotfoot it out of here without hurting her feelings. She doesn't have a clue why I really came up here, so thank God for that. I can give her a friendly, "Nice to see you, we gotta keep in touch," and never have to worry about her again.

But what an idiot I've been. I'm gonna kill Erica when I get back. I almost came real close to hurting a really nice stranger from my past, and it would've been the ultimate pig thing to do. Treat her bad because her face is fucked up. Yeah, nice, write a book about it, tell the world what an asshole you are. Guaranteed number one on Amazon.com.

I leave an alarming amount of blood on the privy's dirt floor, and limp back into the cabin. Adonna's still contentedly eating cereal and brushing away milk leaks as I come back inside.

"That help?"

"Ten minute pee works wonders," I say. She smiles—at least one side of her face does. The skeletor side stays strangely inert. "But I ripped open my foot on the way there," I say, and Adonna comes over to take a look. Must be that nurturing instinct, because before I know it she's got me sitting down with my leg up as she expertly cleans out the wound and bandages it up.

"You're an accident waiting to happen," she says.

"I feel like a spaz," I say, meaning it. "I'm a total feeb, I can't drive off the main highway for ten minutes without one major catastrophe after another."

"I don't think it'll need stitches," Adonna says. "But if it does, I can do it for you. I've got everything here we need."

"I thought I'd head out today," I say. "I've gotta get the Camry towed out and fixed, that'll take time."

"You're not going anywhere," Adonna says. She's smiling, but it's a little different somehow. Forced? I dunno, hard to tell since it's only half a smile. But I don't have time to read between the lines, the only thing I want is outa here.

"You can give me a ride down, can't you?"

"Not anymore. Last night after you passed out we had the biggest thunderstorm I've ever seen. Must've been three inches of rain, washed out the road in a bunch of places. I talked to the HQ, they said it'll take 'em at least a week to bring the D-9 up to grade out the road."

"Oh."

"We could get a med-evac, if you don't mind paying. I doubt your insurance would cover it unless you had a real emergency, though."

"Uh-huh." Shit. This isn't sounding good.

"Of course you could hike out. It's only fifteen miles. But with that foot...."

"What about somebody with an ATV?" I ask. I've seen the commercials, they're supposed to go anywhere.

"You might not have noticed when you came in, but you crossed over the same creek half a dozen times. It's all scoured out now by the flash floods. There's not an ATV in the world that could make it up here. Looks like you're stuck in a ghost town with me." She smiles, I think, and if it wasn't for that hideous side to her face, I'd be smiling back and looking forward to being stranded here.

But I can't. Not like this, not now. Not with Adonna looking like she does.

"Is my backpack around?" I ask. Not that the whole book nonsense matters anymore, but I'd hate to lose the laptop. I might need to pawn it for food.

"Right here," Adonna says, reaching behind the tiny table and lifting it off the floor. She passes it over to me, and as she does she gives me a look. A strange look. I don't know what's up with this. I'm starting to get weird vibes off of her.

I take the backpack and open it.

The laptop's gone.

"Shit."

"What's wrong?"

"My computer's gone."

"No it's not." Adonna gestures to her table. The laptop sits on the far side of the cereal box. "I took it out last night. Didn't want anything to happen to it." She half-grins with that skeleton side overpowering the normal side. I don't say anything. I'm not sure why. Maybe because I have utterly no idea what to say to her. I've used up the chattery small talk, the rehashing of thunderstorms and lightning strikes. It's not like we can reminisce about the past, since we never had one. Now all I'm left with is being stuck in a ghost town with somebody I never really knew who only has half a face.

"You hungry?" she asks.

"Yeah. I guess I am."

In a few moments I'm chowing down the rest of her corn flakes. I usually eat sugar packed garbage like Lucky Charms and Froot Loops, but I'm so ravenous that boring old generic corn flakes taste great. I should look at her, make conversation, but if I look up at that face I'll probably lose my appetite.

I know, I know! You don't have to tell me I'm a prick, I already said I feel guilty, but shit, I can't help it, her... problem...grosses me out. And after all I've been through I need my nutrition, so fuck you. Keep your opinions to yourself; you're not thinking anything I haven't already considered.

But put yourself in my place. You know what I've been through, what an idiot I feel like for even bothering with this bogus-ass scheme, and now that I'm stranded here I've gotta be nice and try not to see her deformity. I'm sorry, I'm just not big enough to be able to deal with it.

If you could see her you'd understand. I've tried to describe it, but you have to see it, the creased scars, quease-inducing color, unnatural expression, the horrible disfigurement...I'll bet if you were in my shoes you wouldn't be any better. Probably just not as honest as me.

Of course, I haven't been totally honest—at least about why I'm here. But why add to her pain? Why make her feel bad? There's no point in that. It'd be cruel, unfair.

It'd be...small. And I'm not small.

Well, I am. But in a different way.

I dunno, I'm rambling, I don't know what to do.

So I inhale corn flakes until I'm about to burst.

"You up to a little hike?" she asks. "I'm have to check out the area, make sure there's no smoldering lightning strikes or anything. It's a nice walk, just a few miles. Do you good."

"Sure," I say, forcing a grin and feigning perkiness. There's nothing I'd rather do less than stomp around in the mountains with her, because I know we'll have nothing to say and I'll feel guilty. But there's no choice.

So in ten minutes we're walking along a rough trail up above Skull Peak. The view of the old town is pretty cool, and although I'm limping and there's no way I can keep up with Adonna, I'm actually enjoying the hike. It takes my mind off other things, and exercise feels good. Every step hurts my foot, though, and even with the expertly applied bandage Adonna set me up with, I'm not going to be able to go very far.

We stop at a granite outcropping high above the town, high above the valley leading down to the main road.

"It's beautiful up here," I say uselessly. I've always hated people who state the obvious, but here I am, being Obvious Man because I don't know what else to say.

"I never get tired of it," she says.

"You ever gonna leave?" I ask.

Adonna gazes far away, her eyes focused on the miles and miles of clear sky, the unfolding mountain valleys and desert beyond. "I don't think so," she says quietly. I'm not the most perceptive guy in the world, but I know what the subtext is. She's saying, "Where else would somebody who looks like me go?"

Now what the hell do I do? This is the problem for me. If I say, "Yeah, sure, I understand" then it's acknowledging her disfigurement, if I say, "Why wouldn't you leave?" well, that's just acting stupid. So for a moment I say nothing. Then, I surprise myself when I ask gently, "What happened to you?"

She gives one of those deep, soul-cleansing sighs. I watch her, her hair blowing in the warm breeze, her strong, bronzed arms clasped around her knees. I'm on the intact side of her face, so from here she looks like what she is—a sad, pretty woman about to tell a sad story.

"I was backpacking with my husband," she says. "Ex-husband now," she adds. "We'd finished a long day, twenty miles of cross-country hiking, and when we finally slogged into the lake we'd decided to camp by we were dead tired. You know how sometimes you're so exhausted it's almost like you're drunk or something? Your brain doesn't do what you want it to, or it fools you into thinking you're fine when you're not...anyway, that night I was like that. Probably had a touch of altitude sickness too, we'd climbed a couple of ridges over twelve thousand feet. Anyway, while Randy was getting water, I got the stove going so we could cook up dinner, and then...I'll never know exactly what happened, but I screwed something up, maybe I dropped the propane cylinder, maybe...I dunno, something happened. Next thing I know my face is on fire and I'm screaming, burning, I've never felt such pain, and Randy came charging up from the lake, but by then, something else had caught fire, my nylon shell, and it flared like a bomb, it stuck to my face and when Randy got there he tried to peel it away but the skin came off with it...." and as she speaks her voice never changes, no emotion, no tears, just like she's reciting some dull statistical report about the economic output of Bulgaria.

"Jesus...." I murmur, and even though it's obvious, in this case it's about all anybody could say.

"I was in shock, of course," she says. "Randy did his best to cover it with wet cloth, and he half carried me out that night. We got back to the road before dawn, and before I knew what was happening I was at UCLA in the burn ward. Got an infection that almost killed me, then lots of plastic surgery."

I don't want to say anything, but if this is what she looks like after plastic surgery, I can't imagine how horrible it was before.

"It's only been a couple of years, and the doctors want to do a bunch more operations...they say they could make me look a whole lot better. Not sure I believe them, though."

"Wow," I say. "That's rough. Did your husband leave....?" It's a nosy question, but since she's talking so openly I figure we're friends, so I might as well ask.

"Yeah. He couldn't take it. Turned out he was kind of weak. He worked for the Forest Service, too. He got a transfer up to Alaska. Said he wanted to get more of a wilderness experience. I knew better. He just didn't want to look at this every day. Can't blame him."

Oh fuck. I want to comfort her, to reassure her. Adonna's so sweet, so honest, and she's been dealt the ultimate bad hand. "I'm really sorry, Adonna."

"It's okay. I'm getting used to the idea of being the way I am. If nothing else, it's truth serum for people. You find out who's decent and who's an asshole," she says.

Guess which side I'm on? She turns to me, the damaged side of her face horrifyingly close, I wish I had the balls to be honest right now, but I force myself to look at her and smile. I suppose in this case dishonesty is the best policy.

"Are you gonna have more surgery?" I ask.

"I'm not sure it's worth the trouble. No matter what, I'm always going to look weird. I may just live with it."

"Up here? Alone?"

"The occasional tourist wanders by, and there's marmots and coyotes and bears...."

"Bears?" I ask, worried. I've always had a fear of big, surly mammals.

"They won't bother you. Unless they smell blood," she says, looking down at my foot.

"Can they smell it through shoes?"

"Never know. Let's go. Just a few more trails, then we'll head back."

I dutifully follow her, my head pivoting at every sound, expecting charging, pissed-off bears to roar in from every direction. But they never do. Just squeaky marmots and the crunch of our own footsteps.

I don't want to whine, but my foot's killing me. And my lungs aren't nearly as efficient as Adonna's. I'm about ready to beg her to carry me back when we round a bend and we're suddenly back in the town. I guess the walk was worth it, because we didn't find any slides or fires or whatever it was she was looking for.

So I'm kind of surprised when I see a big, burly guy standing outside her cabin. I don't see any vehicle, so I can't figure out how he got here. He's leaning against the cabin, picking at his fingernails with a pocketknife. He reminds me of the born-again biker dude who scared me so much at the rest stop. He's like a million other guys you see around, the construction workers or drug dealers or just more...primitive kind of guys—bigger, tougher, grungier—compared to the middle class pansies like me.

"Oh!" Adonna says when she spots him. I guess she'd been staring at her feet or something, because I saw him long before her.

"Somebody you know?" I ask. "Forest Service guy or something?"

Adonna doesn't say anything.

"Hey," the stranger says. A burly, deep voice to go with the barrel chest and huge biceps. How come these guys never have squeaky voices? As we get closer I notice that his bushy beard is unkempt, his long hair greasy. He's wearing mirrored sunglasses, and when he reaches up to take them off the FUCK YOU, ASSHOLE tattoo on his arm flexes alarmingly. He looks me up and down and grins.

Like I'm a chocolate milkshake he's got a craving for.

"You know this guy?" I ask Adonna.

"Yeah," she says.

"Is he gonna kill us?"

"I doubt it."

"Can you give me a guarantee?"

She doesn't answer. She walks over to the scary guy, stands silently before him, then leans in and gives him a huge, spit-swapping kiss. Burly guy puts both his hands on her ass and kneads as he tongues her like they're in a porn video. I'm strangely fascinated that this guy's not the least bit put off by her face.

I guess that makes him a better person than me—if somewhat more disgusting.

I stand, trying not to stare, while they make out. Adonna gets real close to him, and then, as she's on him like melted cheese, she grabs *his* ass and they've got a mutual ass-kneading thing going and I'm feeling a little left out.

I hate to be a pest, but I'm afraid clothes are going to start coming off and they'll be fucking right here, so I give a little courtesy cough to remind them I'm still around.

It has no effect.

So I cough again, louder, with a nice phlegmy gack! to drive home the point.

Burly guy pulls away from the slobbery kisses and narrows a steel-melting glare at me. "You sick, friend?" he asks.

"No, just a little frog in my throat."

Adonna finally realizes she's being rather rude and reluctantly pulls her hands from burly guy's grubby Levi'd ass. She wipes kissy drool from the monster side of her face and smiles at me—at least I think it's a smile, it might be a sneer—and says, "This is Scooter."

"What the fuck kinda name is 'Scooter'?" he asks.

"Nickname," I squeak like the nerdiest eighth grader who ever lived. "You can call me Jimmy."

"How 'bout I don't call you nothing?"

"Sure. No problem."

Adonna laughs like it's the biggest joke in the world. "Scooter, this is

Randy."

The name is familiar, but I can't quite get a grip on why.

"Ex-husband," she adds helpfully.

"Oh," I say.

"I knew Scooter from high school," Adonna says.

"Yeah? So why's he here now?" Randy asks, ignoring me. He's awfully rude.

"Just came to visit," she says. "He got hit by lightning last night."

"No shit," Randy says, looking at me with what seems to be newfound respect. "No wonder he's so fucked up."

This guy's a real gem. It's weird, though, as soon as Adonna saw him, she changed. She was really nice, but now, suddenly, with ex-hubby back, she's tougher, and I'd swear she's sneering at me. I'm wondering if she was just faking being nice and *this* is the real her.

"Be nice, Scooter's cool. He's stranded here till they grade out the roads. You hike in?" she asks.

"Yeah. We gotta..." and then grubby Randy tosses me a withering, none-of-my-business glare and walks off a ways with Adonna. They talk animatedly, he gestures in my direction a few times, and I seriously consider hobbling out of here on my bad foot. Who cares if I'm limping, I don't like the feeling I'm getting from these two. My presence obviously isn't wanted, and I have another vision of killing Erica—if I ever see her again. Have I mentioned that THIS IS ALL HER FAULT!

Okay, what do I do? Get some water, some food, have Adonna bandage up my foot real good, I can hike the fifteen miles to the main road in half a day, hitchhike into town, call Erica, get rescued. I've gotta get out of here, that's for sure. If Randy could hike in, I can hike out, cut foot and all. Shit, it's not like

I'm an invalid or something. I'm a man as much as Randy. Well, maybe not quite as much. But close.

I'm pondering my options when the private confab ends and they wander back over to me.

"Cut your foot, huh?" he says, suddenly solicitous. "You're havin' a shitty couple days. Get hit by lightning, then slice your foot. Gonna have to lay low for awhile till you get healed up."

"I'm thinking maybe I'll go ahead and hike out," I say, expecting a "Yeah, okay, good luck." But that's not what I get.

Instead—

"You'd never make it," Adonna says.

"You ain't goin' nowhere," Randy whispers, and this time any pretence of friendliness is long gone.

"How come—" I start to say.

"It's best that you stay," Adonna interrupts, and it's then that I realize I'm in deep, deep shit....

Chapter Six

When the important choices in life have shown up, I think I've done okay....

I mean, I've never made any really stupid moves, like not wearing a rubber when it was necessary, or refusing to pay taxes, or trying to outrun the cops when a speeding ticket was coming my way.

I'm just an average guy, a rule follower, a sober-minded all-American who just wants to live comfortably and be left alone by authority, bad guys, and religious fanatics.

Just an average guy.

So what the fuck am I doing in a ghost town in the mountains with a damaged ex-classmate and her psycho ex-husband?

Because, oh yeah, Randy is one fucked-up psycho. I'm thinking he's done prison time because he's got that way about him. And it's weird, since he's shown up Adonna has become much tougher...her personality is more like the bad side of her face than the good one.

There's no way this guy was in the Forest Service...he's too nuts, too mean. I doubt he's ever had a real job. Which begs the question: why did Adonna lie to me? And what else is she lying about?

I have to go back a little. Right now I'm trying to sleep while they do God-knows-what over in a shed behind the saloon. They're probably fucking their brains out. Great. I'm shivering in a sleeping bag, my foot throbbing, alarming new tingles beginning to tickle my extremities—I think it must be the lightning getting back at me—while they have sex. Don't I feel like a winner. But I digress. Let's go back to dinner.

I sat at the table in Adonna's cabin, Randy next to me, so close I could smell his stale tobacco-beer breath and sweat. He was hoovering some venison and rice that Adonna whipped up, and I tried to eat but wasn't having much luck. It tasted okay, but my appetite had vanished.

"See, what I'm thinkin' Skeeter," Randy said, venison fragments clinging to his beard, "is that you stay here, lie low and heal until the roads open up. Lie real low, know what I mean?"

"Scooter," I said miserably. "I'm not sure I get you, Randy," I smiled, trying to be affable. I looked to Adonna for help, but all she did was eat and try to keep her dinner from falling out of the dead side of her mouth.

Randy leaned in real close to me. His crazy bloodshot eyes drilled me, and any thought of eating vanished with his hostility. "What you need to do," he said, "is mind your own business. Don't be stickin' your nose where it don't belong."

"No problem," I croaked.

"You enjoy the dinner?" Adonna asked as if her crazy ex- hadn't just threatened me.

"Real good," I said.

"Shot the deer myself," she said proudly.

"Great."

So there we sat. The weirdest dinner I've ever suffered through—and that includes boring Thanksgivings with Jane's family and a horrendous evening spent with a guy and his wife I knew from the paper who invited us over for dinner and spent the whole time trying to convert us to Scientology.

I'm not sure where I am here. I mean in the standing sense, not geographical. Randy scares me to death, and his implied threats have penetrated even my thick head. And Adonna, well, I don't know what's up with her. But I don't know how to proceed. I can't escape, really, but I'm not sure I need to. I don't have enough information to know what to do.

So maybe I should follow Randy's advice. Maybe just lie low, be invisible, until I can get the hell outa here.

So I try to sleep.

And I can't.

Because something's really wrong here. Something bad's going on.

And for a reason I'll never understand no matter how long I live, I suddenly decide I've just *got to know* what it is.

Weird. Because as soon as I decide I'm going to sleuth what's up, I drift off into contented sleep....

It's morning, and Adonna and Randy are nowhere to be seen. I don't think they ever came back to the cabin last night. Now it's time to start looking.

I'm kinda excited about this. It might lead to trouble, but shit, I've never done anything remotely dangerous in my life. Maybe I've got a new perspective since I got hit by lightning... maybe that changed everything forever about Jimmy Biffman. I don't know. Whatever the reason, I feel different this morning. I'm tingly—literally and figuratively—and I want to get out there and snoop.

As I stand there's something really creepy...everything below my knees tingles like my skin is crawling. I remember playing Trivial Pursuit once, and the word was "formication", and it meant the sensation of bugs crawling underneath the skin. I remember thinking it was the creepiest thing I'd ever heard, and now I've got it. Lightning bugs. And I giggle. It's funny, lightning bugs.

Guess you've got to have been hit by lightning to appreciate the humor.

Anyway, it's time to Sherlock and find out what the fuck those two are up to. I could write a fucking mystery, how my hunt for a woman turns into something else, and I end up the hero! Yeah. Perfect.

I go outside. The day is crisp; fall already kisses the mornings. After a hurried pee in the outhouse, I gimp-walk around the dusty streets. This place is really pretty cool, if you take the time to admire and appreciate it. I pretend I can hear the voices from the past, the dancehall girls, drunk miners, fights, noisy life, the crack of—

"HEY ASSHOLE!"

I stop dead. Either one of the miners' ghosts has come back to life to mess with me, or crazy Randy is *really* pissed.

I turn.

Randy stands in the middle of the street, fifty feet away, squinting at me. He's still wearing the same grimy shit he had on last night, and his beard shines greasy in the morning sun.

"Hey, yourself," I smile. I don't know why, but for some reason I'm not so afraid of him anymore.

"I THOUGHT I TOLD YOU TO MIND YOUR OWN BUSINESS!"

It's fun, like an old western movie, facing down the gunfighter on the main street while frightened town folk peer out windows and hope no stray bullets fly their way.

"I am," I say. Which is true, sort of. I hadn't even begun to snoop yet.

"Get back in the fuckin' cabin and stay there!" he blusters, then stomps off into an alley.

I really should do as he says, because the guy can hurt me, but what the hell, I'm in gumshoe mode now, so I follow him.

I tiptoe around, although I don't think there's any reason to, and I duck in doorways, following grubby Randy as he stomps toward an old stable behind a row of boarding houses. Smoke curls from a chimney in the stable—which seems odd to me. Why would a stable have a chimney? There must be a lot about the past that I don't know.

Randy flings open the door and goes inside.

The gray-bleached wooden siding is gapped and sloughing off, revealing glimpses of Adonna and Randy moving about inside. From the kaleidoscope image, they seem to be busy doing something; some kind of chore or work. Definitely not funtime. They're working on something.

I move closer.

That tingly shit in my legs is getting worse, moving up toward my waist, and I wonder how long it'll be before my balls and dick have the sensation. I'm not sure if that'll be pleasant or not.

But none of that matters now, because I'm investigating, snooping, being sneaky, disobeying the creepy mean guy because I'm Jimmy Biffman, P.I.

I skulk to the stable and peer inside a long crack.

I'm puzzled at first. Adonna is cooking something. She and Randy mutter to each other about something, and I can't make out what they're saying.

But as I watch it dawns on me what it is they're doing.

Adonna is cooking a vat of something stinky, a witches brew of chemical shit that vents up the old chimney. Sleazy Randy helps her, and I've watched enough true crime stuff on the upper reaches of the cable channels to know they're whipping up a batch of meth. Speed. Crank.

Oh, man, the ultimate white trash cooking party. Randy I can understand, but Adonna? That's biker shit, it's loser crackers with rotten teeth and trailer trash and backwoods goombahs.

What a disappointment. It's so ordinary, so sleazy. I don't know what I expected; maybe something glamorous, like counterfeiting, or, I don't know, something more interesting than a nightmare cheap drug.

My balls are tingling. It's not from discovery or excitement, it's from the lightning. Oh oh, there goes the dick. *Tingle, tingle, tingle.*

I giggle. I don't know why, I shouldn't, but suddenly there's something amusing about all this. Lightning-dick-tingle-boy watching a couple of losers cook up a batch of speed.

If only Erica could see me now.

But I don't get much time to enjoy my giggling, because Randy hears me and he's charging outside like a bull after the red cape.

"WHAT'D I TELL YOU, MOTHERFUCKER!"

"I dunno, Randy, what the FUCK did you say?"

He's coming toward me, reaching into his greasy leather jacket, and it's now that I get the first real non-lightning tingle, because I realize I've just fucked up big time.

Because I think the asshole's reaching for a gun.

What was I thinking? I'm not normally reckless, did I think I could just mouth off to the guy and nothing would happen? Even if he doesn't shoot me, he's gonna kick my ass.

That lightning bolt must've affected my judgment.

But there's nothing I can do now, so I stand my ground and wait for the inevitable.

Adonna runs out behind him, but with her skeletor face it's hard to tell what her expression really is. She's either smiling that I'm about to get creamed or she's worried that I'm about to get creamed or she doesn't really give a shit because she's gotta get back inside and stir up her witches' brew of poison.

And as Randy's hand emerges from inside the leather jacket, it's the worst possible news. A gun comes out, pointed in my direction, and it's now that I slide into a weird slo-mo feeling, kinda like the flying stuff in *The Matrix*, I feel like I'm moving either really slow or really fast and Randy and Adonna are moving slow, but something's weird, and the lightning tingle is through my whole body—

Randy's screaming at me, waving the gun, but I don't hear anything. Adonna's running up behind him, arms waving, but I don't hear her, either. My eyes are zoom vision and I see Randy's trigger finger and it sure looks like he's tensing it, ready to squeeze it and pump me full of lead.

Full of lead. Great expression, like an old gangster movie.

Cliché boy, that's me. Time for action, though. No time to ponder.

What happens next...well I don't really know what happens next. My tingly left leg kicks, apparently on its own, and then the right, and then the left again, and I sense my feet making contact but it's all blurry and speeded up or slowed down, but before I know what's happened I'm holding Randy's gun.

And then I shoot him in the head.

Over and over and over until the gun is empty and Adonna's screams penetrate into my brain and time gets real and the tingling is less noticeable and I watch the blood leak out of what used to be the top of grungy Randy's dumb, white trash skull....

Chapter Seven

"I think I killed Randy."

"NO SHIT, SCOOTER!" Adonna yells, unnecessarily loud, if you ask me.

The gun is hot and smoky in my hand. I let it fall to the ground.

"I probably shouldn't have done that," I say, preternaturally calm, "but he was trying to kill me. I think it was self-defense."

Adonna is shaking. Randy lies still, the top of his head long gone. His eyes are open, though, in the most startled expression. Like somebody snuck up on him and yelled, "BOO!"

"I should be more upset about this," I say.

Adonna doesn't respond. She's shaking and crying.

"I don't know why I'm not," I continue. And I don't know. I've certainly never killed anybody before—it's not like I'm a hardened murderer. But for some reason I'm not all that bothered. I'm more concerned about the tingle that's now reached into my love handles and belly. A tingling belly is a strange thing. It's not a sensation you ever have.

Unless you've been zapped by lightning and killed a guy.

"You better call somebody," I say. "On your radio. The police."

Adonna stops crying and glares at me. The damaged side of her face looks particularly threatening, animal-like. Vicious.

"We're not calling anybody!"

"But Randy's dead."

"I know that!"

"Don't you think we should call somebody?"

"No!"

I move away from Randy. Those staring eyes are starting to bother me. Not guilt, actually, just that unsettling feeling you get when somebody's looking at you and you'd rather they didn't.

Adonna seems...confused. Unsure what to do. But the tears are quickly lessening, and I sense that her mind is working. She steps over Randy and picks up the gun. She points it at me.

"There's no bullets left," I say.

She shakes her head disgustedly and throws the gun at me. I side-step it and it clatters against some rocks.

"Fucking Scooter," she says. "Why'd you ever come here?!"

"Just one of those things," I say. I decide suddenly to tell her the truth. "Actually, I came to—"

"I know why you came!" she snaps.

"You do?"

"I read your little love story on the computer the night you got hit by lightning. I know all about you and that freak Erica and your stupid plan to...what was it, 'Jimmy's search for the perfect woman?' Well here I am, Scooter, your perfectly fucked-up woman!"

I wonder why she asked why I came here when she already knew? She must be upset about Randy. This is so weird, I can't make myself give a rat's ass about the guy even though I offed him. So strange. So much has changed. *Tingle, tingle, tingle.* Pretty soon it'll be up to my nipples.

"What're we gonna do, Adonna?"

She shakes her head and stomps off back into the stable, probably to turn down the pot o' meth before it blows up. Flies already buzz around Randy's head, and I move away. There's nothing more to do or say or feel at this point, so I go back to Adonna's cabin.

My foot's throbbing. It hurts even through the tingle. I hope it's not infected with that flesh-eating bacteria you read about, where a guy pops a butt zit and before he knows it they've cut off his legs and are heading for his arms.

I guess I'm selfish. At least I'm still alive.

Unlike Randy.

Randy.

And now, suddenly, I begin to shake. The gravity of what I've done hits me hard, a sucker punch to the kidney, and I'm afraid of what might happen. What if Adonna lies, what if she says I murdered Randy? They were the criminal pals, the crank partners, I was just the fool who blundered into their lives. Oh shit, I'm dead, or at least going to prison. Love Slave Scooter, I can see it already, bent over a prison bunk while the *really* guilty have their way with me.

Oh shit, mother of God, I've gotta get the hell outa here.

I stuff my backpack with my meager belongings, I should bandage my foot but there's no time, gotta hit the road, and as I rush to the door and fling it open—

Adonna waits on the other side.

"Going somewhere?"

I drop the backpack at her feet. The tingles are at my chest, it's like my nipples are alive, my heart pounds, *MY GOD, I KILLED A GUY!*

"Lemme outa here, Adonna!"

"We need," she says, very calm now. "We need to stick together from here on out."

"I don't think—"

"You don't know anything about anything. We're a team whether you like it or not."

I can't say anything. My chin's starting to tingle.

"You've found your dream woman, Jimmy," she says quietly.

I've never dug a grave before.

Adonna and I hack into the rocky soil outside of town, through layers of rubble and knobby roots and the detritus of the previous inhabitants.

"This was were they dumped their trash," Adonna says, going into park ranger mode. I half expect her to invite me to a slide show later explaining the sanitation practices of our great-great-great whatevers a hundred years ago.

"Why can't we just put him in a mineshaft?" I ask. I'm not feeling very spunky at the moment. My foot throbs and everything else from head to toe tingles. Even my hair follicles are alive with electricity. I'm beginning to wonder if this lightning tingle will be with me forever. I don't know if I can get used to the feeling.

"Because somebody might find him."

"Who, ghosts?"

"It's a bad idea. Burying is more permanent."

"If you say so."

She clangs her shovel against a rock and glares at me. "I *do* say so!"

"Fine. But other than burying the guy without a permit, or whatever you need, there's no crime here. I didn't do anything wrong. It was total self-defense." I sound like one of those NFL thugs who get arrested every so often after they blow away an old girlfriend.

"There's a lot you don't know," Adonna says, and for the first time since I blew off her ex-husband's head, she sounds nice again, friendly almost. And a little sad. Probably about dead Randy.

"He was married to you once? Or was that a lie?" I ask. Might as well find out.

"Yeah, we were married. Until the accident."

"The hiking thing?" I ask.

"Randy never hiked a day in his life."

"So what happened?"

"I was a crankhead, so was he. I met him in a bar, we got married for some reason I'll never know, and when we were making up a batch it went bad and I got burned. End of story."

"Oh."

"But a back-to-nature backpacking accident is a little more socially acceptable, don't you think? Especially to an old high school guy who's looking for a mate."

"That all seems pretty stupid now."

"It was stupid when you started. What would make you do something like that?" she asks, as if we're digging a hole for a plant and not her dead ex.

"I dunno. My wife dumped me, Erica got this idea and I sorta went along."

"Now you've got a good story," Adonna says, clanking her shovel against a rock and sending out a mini-shower of sparks.

"I don't care about the story," I say, rubbing my electric scalp. Shit, this is a weird sensation.

"Good. I'd hate to see you...write it down."

"Why?"

"Why do you think, asshole?" she snaps.

"Oh."

"Yeah. 'Oh'. We're gonna be a team for awhile, I think."

"Listen, after we get Randy buried, whataya say we just go our separate ways, okay? I won't say a word to anybody, you don't say anything, we get on with our lives."

"I don't think so."

"Why not?"

"I want a fresh start," Adonna says.

"That's what I'm saying!"

She tosses down her shovel. "That's deep enough. Let's go get him."

I follow her over to Randy's body. Those flies are still buzzing, and a curious marmot chirps accusingly from the rocks.

"Pick him up," Adonna says.

I look down at him. The blood has congealed; his eyes are cloudy but still staring. My tingles start tingling.

"I'm not touching a dead guy."

"Jesus fucking Christ," Adonna mutters. She goes into the stable, comes out with a wheelbarrow, and horses Randy into it herself. His arms and legs dangle limply over the side.

"Help me push him," she says, her voice dripping with "You're a pussy" accusation. I can't help it, I *am* a pussy. What I wouldn't give right now to be home, or at least in Eric and Erica's trailer, collecting unemployment and watching a rugby match on ESPN 2.

We clumsily make our way to Randy's grave. He almost flops out of the wheelbarrow, but we jerk it back upright before he goes. When we get to the hole we unceremoniously dump him in. He's face down, and from this angle you can't really see that his head's been damaged. He looks like a guy sleeping on his stomach.

It's very strange covering him up. Like burying, well, garbage. Or a pet. I had to bury one of Crystal's cats that had been squashed into a road Frisbee, and this has the same feeling.

Although I was much more fond of the cat.

We silently finish the job. And then we stand there, catching our breath.

"What now?" I finally ask.

"We're gonna hit the road."

"I don't think—"

"You don't have a choice. If you don't stay with me, I call the cops and turn you in. They'll believe a forest ranger. What's a detective gonna think about your 'looking for a woman' story? All I say is you came up here, were acting weird, then you shot Randy because you thought he was a threat to your...plan."

"You wouldn't do that."

"Try me," she says. And I believe her.

Oh shit.

"Why do you want me with you?" I ask.

"Shits and giggles," she says. "Hope your foot doesn't hurt too much, 'cause we're hiking outa here."

Every step feels like my foot is ripping apart. Hot searing stabs shoot up my leg, and the head-to-toe tingling doesn't cancel it out.

We've only gone a mile or so, but already I'm thinking I won't make it. I wonder if Adonna will leave me here to die? She'll probably bury me like Randy, except with even less warmth of feeling.

"Didn't you feel bad about what happened to Randy?" I ask. She's stomping along the loose granite crumbles ahead of me, and she doesn't bother to stop or turn around.

"If you hadn't shot him, somebody else would've. He was overdue for killing."

"Sentimental, aren't you?"

She says nothing and we stomp onward.

I've gotten over the panic of killing somebody. Now I'm more interested—or worried—about my own problems, physical and with the law. This tingling shit and the foot and the guilt—it all mixes together into a queasy mush of nauseating fear.

"Where you planning on going?" I ask.

"Dunno."

"I assume you're quitting the Forest Service. Shouldn't you write a letter or something?"

"They'll figure it out."

"When we get to the road, I'm calling the police and we're gonna put a stop to all this. They'll believe me," I say with somewhat less than complete conviction.

"Is that what you really want?" Adonna asks. She stops and faces me.

And through the tingling and pain and guilty fear, something strange hits me, a feeling of exhilaration, of...danger. But not scary. Invigorating.

Maybe it's the day. A cool wind whips among the peaks, a hawk glides far above us, riding the thermals, marmots squeak, the sky is so blue it hurts, even Adonna's hair blows wispy strays that dance appealingly across the undamaged side of her face.

There's something magic right now. Something between us. Maybe it's guilt, maybe because we shared in something skullduggerous, but I'm suddenly not sure I want to split off from her. Maybe I should hang with her awhile and see what happens.

Am I fucked up or what?

"I didn't think so," she says, reading my tingly, weird-ass face. "You want a thrill, Scooter. You're off to a good start. Most people don't ever kill another human being."

"It was self defense," I whisper.

"Doesn't matter. You've crossed a line now. Don't you want to keep going? Think of all the fun stuff you can write and tell little Erica about. I'll bet she'll think you're really something special when you tell her about your adventures with Adonna."

What's she doing? "Stop fucking with me."

She grins. "Let's go, Scooter. We've got adventures ahead of us."

I follow her.

My foot hurts, my tingles tingle, but I'm following her.

Thinking about what she said.

What about Erica? With the excitement of the last thirty-six hours, I haven't thought much about her. Maybe I won't even bother contacting her again. Ever. It seems now like my old life—Scooter Biffman, sports ace, husband, Crystal's dad, Eric and Erica's pal—it's like he never existed, or he's just somebody I read about. It's like that life is already so far removed from where I am now it's just a vague dream.

And Erica, she's so far away from this, from Adonna, from dead Randy, from lightning-struck me, I don't know if I can ever, well, connect with her again.

Too much has happened.

So I follow Adonna.

My foot numbs; I hope that's a good sign. The day warms to hot, and the high altitude sunrays beating down on my forehead feel good.

We pass by the hulk of my old Camry. Strange. I'm thinking of it in past tense, like it's completely dead, no longer mine. All it needs is a new oil pan, but I don't care. I don't want it anymore.

"What'll happen to it?" I ask as we leave it behind us.

"Who cares?"

Yeah. Who cares?

"Do you have any idea where you want to go, Adonna?"

"Nope. You?"

"Nope."

"Good. We'll go there together."

Fuckin' A, I hate to admit it—

But this feels good.

Chapter Eight

I'm so sick of Jesus I could scream.

It's Tuesday night, and I'm suffering through yet another interminable evening of bible study, led by Pastor Ernie. Pastor Ernie's toupee sits crookedly on his head like a crouching animal, ready to leap at innocent passersby and bite their earlobes.

I look over at Eric. He eagerly gobbles every holy word from Pastor Ernie's mouth. Eric thinks Pastor Ernie is a direct conduit to Jesus. He forgets that Pastor Ernie is a plumbing contractor by day—one who, rumor has it, overcharges for fixing leaky toilets and water heaters.

"Now in Corinthians fourteen-two," Pastor Ernie blathers, thumbing through his wrinkled, saggy old bible, "we see that the Lord...."

Whatever. I tune out.

I don't think I even believe in God anymore. Especially not one who talks to me through an in-denial-bald, dishonest plumber.

What am I going to do? My life is...I don't know.

It's boring. I'm tired of Eric, and, God forgive me, tired of the kids. They're good kids as kids go, and little Eli and Elishaba make me laugh. The rest of them, too, I love them in the way that only mothers can understand, that fierce, take-a-bullet love that leaves me awake at night worrying about them, that makes me cry because I love them so much, that makes me hate Eric because he keeps insisting that I have more.

I could say no, I suppose. But I've been cowed enough by Eric that I submit. "Wives be submissive to your husbands," and all that. At first I was head-over-heels with the born-again stuff, even more than Eric. And it was strange: the holier we got, the more erotically charged our marriage became. We were on fire toward each other, drunk with passion and lust and love of Jesus, we made love constantly, wonderfully, and I had baby after baby after baby.

And then the fires started to flicker.

It was inevitable, and I guess we were luckier than most. The passion lasted far longer than our friends—than poor Scooter. Jane was a cold fish from the start. I used to accuse Scooter of being the only young married couple I knew who slept in twin beds. Scooter laughed, but it was a tight laugh, and I wondered if they ever had sex.

But then Crystal came along, and unless she was a product of a white dove flapping around over Jane's bed, Scooter had at least gotten hold of Jane once. But I never saw any fire between them. They reminded me of business partners.

That's how Eric and I have ended up. We flamed out, and then there was nothing left except a bunch of kids and endless hours praying, listening to losers like Pastor Ernie, and dreaming about eternal salvation and dying and going home to Jesus.

Which I don't think I believe anymore.

How did I get to this point?

Scooter's so lucky. Right now he's living a dream, out there trying to find his perfect woman.

I wish I was him.

When he called last night from the fleabag hotel in the middle of nowhere with the noisy neighbors having wild sex, I was envious. Envious that Scooter was having an adventure, envious that those people next door sounded like they were having such fun, envious that every minute Scooter faced was a minute that he didn't know where he was headed.

Adventure. Mystery.

I hate him.

He's so lucky.

Pastor Ernie is driving home a point, and our sweaty little congregation nods seriously. Some silently mouth prayers and "Amens". I study our peers. There's Dot, the retired barmaid Eric "saved" when he was delivering beer to the tavern she worked at. And there's Dennis and Maggie, a couple our age who are the most humorless grouches I've ever known. I realize as I look around the room that I don't really like anybody here. Eric included.

Even me.

How did I get here?

I spend my evenings and Sundays and every waking hour soaked in Jesus and the bible and redemption and I'm the most unredeemed person on the planet. I teased Scooter the other night, scared him to death with giggly non-sense about dumping Eric, and I probably shouldn't have, but I think if he'd said the word I would've run off with him and left the kids and Eric behind. I cried in the bathroom that night, locked behind the door with the water running so Eric wouldn't hear my sorry betrayal, my weakness, my sins.

But now, after thinking about it, I don't know. Maybe I'd still leave if I had the chance. Maybe not.

Deserting your family is probably about the biggest sin there is this side of murder—would I have the guts? The selfishness to pull it off? I don't know. I just don't know.

Maybe I should find out.

When I get up and leave the room nobody notices. Even though I climb over Eric I don't think he's aware. He's got that faraway Jesus look in his eye I know so well. He gets caught up in devotion, and the real world disappears. I think he fantasizes about heaven the way most men dream about blowjobs.

There I go again. Thinking something like that will throw me into hell forever.

But right now, as I climb into the minivan and start it up, I don't care. I hope Eric understands. I hope the kids understand. I'll call them. Or write a letter. It kills me that I'm abandoning my children, and the thought of little Eli and Elishaba without me.

I wipe the guilty tears from my cheek. I wipe away my life.

And then I drive off into the night.

I'm gonna go find Scooter.

"Mommy?"

Eli's voice on the phone is a bullet in the heart. I don't know if I can speak.

"Hi, sweetie. Can I talk to Daddy?"

I try to keep the shaking out of my voice, because kids are sensitive to stuff like that, but I think Eli notices.

"When are you coming home?" he asks in his high little innocent voice.

I start to speak when there's a thumpy commotion over the phone lines and Eric's voice cracks over the earpiece, harsh and angry and accusatory and...scared.

He sounds insanely frightened.

"Where are you?!" he whispers.

"Listen Eric—"

"Where *are* you?!"

"I had to get away for awhile."

"What about the kids? What about me?!"

"What about *me*?" I ask.

"It's not about you, Erica. I realize things haven't been as good between us as they used to, but it was just God's way of testing us, and you flunked!"

"Am I going to hell, Eric?"

A long silence. I smile. I know him so well. He's thinking "YES!" but he doesn't want to say it.

"It's okay," I say. "I need time to think. I don't know how long I'll be gone."

"But the kids...."

"I know," I say, stifling a sob. I'm so torn. I've been gone twelve hours and already the ache of my motherhood is so painful I can hardly breathe.

But I need to get away.

"This is the only way I can survive. If I don't find out—"

"Find out what?!"

"I dunno. I won't know until I find it."

"You're talking like you're nuts, are you on drugs? Is there someone else?"

"No."

"This is Satan's doing. You know how clever he is. He plants doubts, fills you with deception and lies. Have you prayed?"

"No Eric, I haven't prayed." Sigh. Now he's starting to bore me. If I need reassurance that I'm doing the right thing, talking to Eric is providing it.

"Pray with me."

"No."

"'Oh most heavenly Father, help your daughter Erica see that abandonment isn't the answer to her worries. Cast Satan from her spirit—'"

It's a nice little prayer. Eric is very good at off-the-cuff prayer ditties, and I suppose it's rude to hang up on him in the middle of it, but listening to Eric is like listening to Pastor Ernie, and well, there's just no point. Besides, I'm afraid Eli might come back on the line and that would truly break my heart. If Eric was smart he'd have put some of the kids on the phone and I probably wouldn't have had the willpower to stay away.

But now, strangely, after talking to Eric and listening to his pathetic holiness, I'm renewed, refreshed, reassured that I'm doing the right thing.

I gas up the minivan and head off to find Scooter. I don't know what I'll do when we meet up, but I'll play it by ear. I'm not even sure if Scooter's right for me. If I'd thought so we might've gotten together back in high school.

But I want in on his freedom. I want a piece of the action, whatever it may be.

* * *

The miles flash by on the odometer, and the beautiful country unfolds before me. I'm out in the middle of the desert, not far from the town that Scooter called me from, near the hotel where those people were having such great sex.

I feel so...mixed. Part of me is free, giddy with excitement and freedom, and the other part is black guilt dragging me down so far I don't know if I can ever come up.

But I've got to finish what I've started, even though I don't know what that will mean. I realize I'll probably go back home. I can't leave the kids forever. But for now, maybe a few days, weeks, whatever, I'm going to try to find...something.

"Can't get up there just now," the doofus ranger is telling me. I wonder if this guy talked to Scooter? I'll bet Scooter just loved him.

"Why not?"

"Road's washed out. And we can't get hold of Adonna. We're not sure what's up. Radio's probably busted."

Hmmm.... Are Adonna and Scooter too busy to be answering a radio call?

I'm not sure how I feel about that.

"I need to find my friend."

The dopey ranger theatrically rubs his chin, like he's thinking over an incredibly difficult problem.

"You could probably ride out with the work crew that's grading the road. They could get you pretty close, then you could hike the rest of the way."

"Fine. Let's do it."

The goof smiles, and I'd swear he's flirting with me. So I flirt back; it feels good to be flirted with. None of the church people would dare, and besides,

I'm usually towing kids along wherever I go. The ranger may be a geeb, but at my stage of life anything is better than nothing.

"Thanks," I say, breathy.

He blushes.

That I still possess feminine power is intoxicating.

By the time I trudge into the nasty old ghost town, I'm sweaty and tired and anything but sexy. I rode on a big tractor road grader thingie with a fat guy named Bud. He was nice, and we talked about nothing for awhile, but I was too keyed-up to be very social. By the time he let me off I was so pumped up I almost ran the rest of the way. I slowed down at Scooter's car—it seemed strange that he left it there but it looked like something was broken—and I pressed on into Skull Peak. Now I'm here and nobody else is.

Adonna and Scooter are gone.

I wander around calling out their names, yelling, my voice bounces off the peaks, but no response other than birds and fat little things that look like gophers on steroids.

Wonderful. Now what?

It's already late afternoon, and I doubt I could get back down to Bud and hitch a ride out, so it looks like I'll be spending the night in a ghost town.

And as soon as I think that thought, I smile. A night alone up in the mountains in a ghost town. Damn. Grrrrl Power! I'm doing something...dangerous, crazy. Instead of sitting around listening to Pastor Ernie—or pretending to listen to his Corinthians deconstruction—I'm living a daring life. So different, so—cool!

I explore the old buildings. It's creepy here. I keep expecting people, because when you're in a town with buildings and streets and everything, your mind expects to see people. It's like one of those nuclear holocaust movies from the '50s, where a few survivors would wander around the deserted city and quickly lose their minds.

It's now that the place really starts to get to me. The wind whistling through broken boards, silence too silent, spooky shadows and darting movements I swear I see out of the corner of my eye, but when I turn there's nothing there.

Okay, steady yourself. Don't be stupid. It's an old town, nobody's here, you're gonna have to sleep here tonight, then tomorrow you go down and find Bud and get a ride out and then—

What?

I don't know. I'll have to sleep on it.

I'm pushing open the door to a saloon when something makes a soft *whisk* sound behind me and I don't bother to look back because I assume it's just a gust of wind but when the voice says, "Hi," I jump and if my skin wasn't firmly attached it would be a quivering flesh-covered pile right next to me.

"Oh!" I say, spinning around.

"Sorry," a tall, nice-looking guy says. "I didn't think anybody else was here."

"Neither did I," I gasp. My heart's thumping like it's going to blast out of my chest.

"Didn't mean to scare you," he says. He's got a faint Southern drawl; he's tanned and tough and handsome. Long, long eyelashes. How come the guys always get the lashes and we have to get by with thin, spindly wisps?

"You didn't," I say, but my shaky voice betrays me. He smiles. His teeth are perfect, like a rich person's.

"Are you a tourist?" he asks.

"No. Are you?"

Handsome guy grins wider. He reminds me of an in-shape construction worker. You know the type. Most of them are flabby and fat, with big butt cleavage and dull, stupid eyes. But not this guy. He's one the girls would watch while he poured cement or hammered nails. Sort of like the construction guy who used to be in the Village People, except probably not gay.

"Nah. I'm not a tourist. I'm looking for some friends."

"Me too. Well, just one friend."

"Adonna?" he asks, surprised.

"Sort of. I know—knew her. And Jimmy Biffman."

Handsome guy shakes his head. "Don't know him. You and this Jimmy friends of Adonna and Randy?"

"Who's Randy?"

And now handsome guy's smile gets a little tight, like he's not sure what's going on and he doesn't completely trust me. While he's sizing me up, I size him up. He's wearing jeans, pointy cowboy boots, a thick flannel shirt and jacket. He could pass for a cowboy, I suppose, but there's something city about him. I'm not sure what. Sophistication? Or maybe just that cold look you see in the guy in the next car when you're sitting in gridlock on the freeway.

"They don't seem to be around," he says.

"Nope."

He reaches into his coat and pulls out a pack of Marlboros. He taps one out and holds up the pack. "Smoke?"

I've never smoked in my life. I've always thought it was vile, stupid, that only weak-willed sinners who didn't mind defiling their godly temple—that's one of Eric's favorite expressions—would light up. And I hate the smell of smoke and the arrogant way smokers flick their spent butts all over the place and, and, and....

"Sure," I say, taking it. Oooooh, so dangerous. What a bad girl. I almost giggle. Good thing there's not a tattoo parlor around.

Handsome guy flicks a lighter and holds it under the tip. I inhale enough to get it started, but don't dare suck any smoke into my lungs. I might throw up on his boots and that would definitely *not* be cool.

"So," he says, exhaling a fogbank of Marlboro into my face. "Seems like we're looking for ghosts."

"It's a ghost town," I say lightly, but then I realize I sound like a dork. Once a band fag, always a band fag.

"Yeah," he says blandly, apparently having the same thought.

"So," I say, puffing on the cigarette. A stray smoke wisp finds its way into my lungs and I stifle choke/coughs.

"Doesn't make a lot of sense that they're not here," he says.

"You never told me your name. I'm Erica."

"Nice to know you. I'm Jimmy. Just like your friend."

"That's easy to remember." I say it with a stupid giggle, and God, I sound like a complete idiot. Have I been holy Erica so long I've forgotten how to have a normal conversation with a stranger? I've been sheltered by Eric and the church forever; I realize I haven't actually talked to somebody new for ages. And this Handsome Jimmy, he's got some danger about him. I like it.

I like talking to him. Here. In the deserted ghost town. And it looks like we've got a mystery on our hands.

"Where would they have gone?" I ask.

"Doesn't make much sense to me," Handsome Jimmy says. "They promised me they'd be here. I'm wonderin' if your Jimmy might've got in the middle of something he didn't belong in."

My exhilaration instantly turns to fear. The blue eyes beneath those long lashes suddenly are devoid of feeling. Cold. Dead shark eyes.

"He was just dropping by to say hello," I say carefully.

"And then you're here, too. Seems strange," he says, smiling. But it's not a friendly smile.

"I just...I just came after Scooter—my friend Jimmy—to see, to take a little break from my family."

"Got a family do you, Erica?"

"Yes."

"How many little ones?" he asks, back to being the friendly handsome guy. But I'm cautious now. Something's not right with him.

"Seven."

"You been busy. Don't look old enough to have so many kids."

A soft breeze blows between us, clear and sweet and mountainy. I'm confused. The little fear surge is still with me, but so is the excitement of being out here. They're fighting each other, my common sense and fear duking it out with the wildly exciting rush of doing something dangerous.

"Who's Randy?" I ask.

"Adonna's husband. Or ex-, I guess. Not sure. They were talking about busting up permanently, but I don't know that they ever did."

Handsome Jimmy glances around. He's losing interest in talking, I can tell. He has the same distracted air about him that I do when the kids are chattering and all I'm doing is throwing in an occasional, "Uh-huh."

"What now?" I ask.

He takes a long drag on the Marlboro, grins, then drops it on the ground and grinds it out with his boot.

"I'm thinking, Erica, that we need to find 'em."

"I'll probably head home."

"We'll have to go looking. I know some places," he says, as if he hasn't heard.

"Well, good luck. Tell my Jimmy to call me when you find them." I turn and walk away, even though it's too late to get a ride back to the road. I don't know what I'll do, but I know I can't stay here with this guy. Imagined danger is one thing. This might be real.

"You plannin' on sleeping with the coyotes tonight? Gonna be dark soon, you'll never get back to the road."

"I'll be fine." The gravel crunches behind me as he walks quickly to me. I half expect him to grab me, or maybe a gunshot or something horrible. But all he does is come up beside me, match strides, and light another Marlboro.

"I'd feel real bad if anything happened to you. I'll walk back with you."

"That's okay."

"You oughta stay here tonight. Make a whole lot more sense. We can head back first thing in the morning. You parked down at the road?"

"Yeah."

"Okay then. You can sleep in Adonna's cabin, I'm sure she's got food in there. We can have a nice dinner, you'll be warm. I'll sleep...somewhere. Shoot, got the whole town to chose from."

He suddenly sounds so reasonable, so friendly. I stop walking. My Marlboro has fizzled out; it dangles sadly from my lips. But it feels so...cool to have a smoke dangling. I'm like a femme fatale in a movie. Handsome Jimmy locks my eyes with his baby blues, he's not scary anymore, just a nice guy who's concerned that I'm walking off into the mountains to get eaten by a giant beaver or something.

Maybe I've got him wrong. My people sensor is whacked out; I never use it anymore. Maybe I read him wrong, when I sensed danger he was just annoyed that he came all the way up here and his friends were gone. I feel that way, too. I'd sure like to know where Scooter is.

The sun dips behind the peaks, and it's suddenly chilly. As if on cue a coyote howls in the distance, a hawk goes squawking overhead, one of those fat rodents squeaks, and Handsome construction-worker-dreamboat Jimmy smiles at me.

Looks like I'm spending the night in a ghost town with a mysterious stranger.

"Good old Adonna," Handsome Jimmy says, grinning. He pours me a shot of Wild Turkey. "She's always prepared."

We've just finished eating a batch of noodles he whipped up—well, I call them noodles, everybody else says pasta—and he even made up a pretty good sauce from some cans of tomatoes and spices Adonna had. I sip the booze—this is weird, I can't tell you the last time I had a drink. Even though Eric is a beer distributor, we don't partake in our house, and we especially don't partake of hard liquor. I giggle inside at the thought of Eric's reaction if he knew I was boozing it up with a good-looking stranger in a ghost town.

The dinner was nice. We ate, had some pleasant conversation, nothing deep, nothing scary, nothing relating to why Adonna and her husband and Scooter aren't here.

We just chatted. Like people who've just met, who are sitting next to each other on a flight across country and are just chatting. Normal. It feels weird to be normal.

It got a little strange when I asked Handsome Jimmy what he did for a living. "Investments," was all he said. Very cryptic, and a lie, I'm sure. But I didn't mind. If he didn't want to tell me, it wasn't any of my business. Besides, even though things were okay—I wasn't scared—I was still pretty sure that there was something nefarious about him, something edgy.

I let the burning hot liquid lie on my tongue, then swallow it. Like the cigarette, I'm not up to the challenge, and I cough.

"You like that?" Handsome Jimmy asks, smiling. He's really cute when he smiles.

"Don't drink much," I gasp. I wait a second, then figure what-the-hell and down some more. This gulp doesn't burn quite so much.

"Me neither," he says. "Just a little now and then."

It's getting cold. I'm so glad I didn't walk back to the road. I'd be freezing right now, probably hypothermic, wondering what in the world I'm doing out here, instead of cozy in Adonna's cabin drinking Wild Turkey with handsome, dangerous Jimmy.

He throws another log into Adonna's pot-bellied stove. The orange sparks dance madly and fly up the stovepipe like angry bugs and oh the alcohol has hit my brain and I'm feeling it now....

"More please," I say, holding out my suddenly empty glass. Handsome Jimmy grins and pours.

"Seem to be developing a taste for it," he says.

"Yep," I say. My tongue feels thick and separate, like somebody's stuffed a spare into my mouth.

We drink and talk and I think I'm giggling a lot but I'm not sure what about, and Handsome Jimmy tells me something, stories about his past maybe, and I'm not sure what he's saying, maybe something about prison, but I'm giggling and laughing and drinking another glass and boy it sure is getting hot in here and I'm telling him about Eric and the kids and maybe I start to cry because I miss my babies but I don't miss Eric and I drink some more and then everything is sideways and Handsome Jimmy is on the ceiling and I'm on the floor and then I don't feel so good and I'm yelling for Eli and Elizabeth and Elishaba and the rest of them and then I think I'm throwing up and then everything goes black....

Chapter Nine

"Jesus have mercy on my soul...." I moan. I've died overnight, and now I'm knocking at the pearly gates. Where's St. Peter? Where's Jesus? Where's everybody? I'm in pain—oh so much pain—and nobody's here to greet me? I thought dying stopped the pain? Oh God, I'm not in heaven, I'm in hell and *HERE COMES SATAN!*

"How you doin'?" Satan asks.

I'm afraid to open my eyes.

"I don't want to suffer eternal torment," I say, eyes slammed tightly shut. Funny, death has made me religious again, although it's probably too late to do any good.

"Neither do I," Satan says. It sounds like he's smiling. Figures. Eric and Pastor Ernie always said that Satan was attractive and tempting. I always pictured him as looking something like Mel Gibson, except taller. Now I'm about to find out.

A stabbing pain shoots through my head. Did the Master of Darkness just hit me with that pitchfork thingie he carries around? This is going to be worse than I thought...if I'm dead and can still feel pain, it means that hell is everything they say it is, and probably more.

I'm going to have to live with this all because I wanted to walk on the wild side with Scooter. God have mercy on my miserable soul.

And when I realize that my babies won't have their mother, well, then I just break down and cry. Hot tears leak out of my tightly shut eyes, and I'm surprised that I feel them trickle on my cheeks. This doesn't seem right, seeing as how I'm dead and all.

"What's wrong?" Satan asks, and he sounds genuinely concerned. Most un-Satan-like.

"My babies...." I wail, and the pounding in my head gets stronger.

"What about them?" Satan asks.

"They need their mother."

"You'll be back home in no time," Satan says, and I'm starting to think that maybe I'm not in hell after all.

I try to open my eyes. The light is blinding, blurry, and it hurts. Satan must really be stabbing me because my head feels like it's going to explode.

It's then that Handsome Jimmy slowly comes into focus. The ghost town. Dinner.

Drinking.

Ohmygod, I'm the biggest idiot on the planet. I got drunk and now I'm hung over. The only Satan is in my stupid, dopey head.

"You had quite a time last night," Handsome Jimmy smiles.

I slowly sit up. I'm on the cot in Adonna's cabin. I do a quick body inventory: clothes are as I remember, nothing feels weird, like Handsome Jimmy took advantage of me or anything. Can't help being careful.

"I'm not used to drinking," I say, head in hands. Oooooh, I feel lousy.

"No kidding?" Handsome Jimmy smiles. "Not that it'll do any good, but I made some coffee. I've always found the only thing that cures a hangover is lots of time. I was sick for a week once after a really good one," he says. "Kinda like the flu. Think I killed half my brain cells that time," he continues with a dreamy grin like the memory is something wonderful.

A nausea wave starts in my gut and radiates to every part of my body. I double over and dry heave. Handsome Jimmy pats me on the back.

As I retch and shiver and wonder how horrible I look I decide that Handsome Jimmy's a very nice guy. I doubt Eric would be as thoughtful...of course, if I was sick from being drunk he'd probably be doing an exorcism on me instead of offering comfort.

After the innards thunderstorm passes, I stand on shaky feet. "Is there water?" I ask. I can't remember from last night whether or not this place has plumbing.

"Outhouse. There's a bucket over there," he gestures to the metal counter. I douse my face in the freezing water, then stagger outside to the outhouse. I'm not sure why; I don't have to pee or anything, it's just that when you feel this bad the bathroom—or outhouse—is where you want to be.

I try to notice that's it's a beautiful day, but I can't get it to register. I feel too rotten.

As soon as I enter the outhouse I realize it was a dreadful mistake, because the odor of long-forgotten craps hits me like stinky fists and I immediately heave discolored liquid from deep in my bowels. Ohmygod, I'll never drink again.

Finally, after what seems like years, the gut spasms stop and I'm worn out. No more heaves are left, there's nothing else to expel.

I look at myself in a cracked mirror hanging crookedly on the outhouse wall. Purplish circles under my eyes, matted hair, scary-red eyes...the bible's right, sin catches up with you.

I try to repair myself as best I can, but it's a lost cause. I'm no Cindy Crawford, but I do care about my looks. Except now there's no reason to bother. It takes time—Handsome Jimmy said that about getting over the hang-over. Maybe someday I'll look like myself again.

When I get back to the cabin Handsome Jimmy is contentedly eating a bowl of cereal and sipping coffee. He really is a handsome guy, although a week ago if I'd seen him on the street I would've been intimidated. It's that danger thing. He looks like trouble.

Funny. Doesn't bother me now.

I silently sip coffee, and then tentatively have some corn flakes. I'm pleasantly surprised that I don't explosively puke it back up. I guess I'll survive. When I look up from my bowl Handsome Jimmy is watching closely with a small smile.

"Gonna survive?"

"It's touch and go, but I think there's a chance."

"Good. Soon as you're done we need to head out."

And with that he's up and out the door. I hurriedly finish eating and wonder what in the world's going to happen next....

The exercise is doing me good.

We hike down the rocky road, out of Skull Peak and back toward the main highway and my car, and I don't feel so bad. With every step the cobwebs clear and brain pain stabs lessen, and after an hour I'm feeling alive again.

It's hard to stay with Handsome Jimmy, though, because his legs are so long that my puny little strides can't keep up. We have to scramble over the washed-out parts of road, and I keep expecting to run into the construction guys until I realize that it's Sunday.

Sunday.

I should be sitting in the sweltering little church, singing hymns and listening to Pastor Ernie. I should be "Sshh"-ing the kids and exchanging meaningful Jesus glances with Eric. We do that a lot. When Pastor Ernie makes an especially good point, something about salvation or evil Democrats, Eric and I exchange *the glance.* For most normal married couples *the glance* would be used for sexual innuendoes or something playful like that, but in our family *the glance* is reserved for hellfire bible quotes or condemnation of Satan-filled feminist abortionist murderers.

A guilty stab of mother abandonment sneaks in with the dulling hangover stabs. I'm a rotten mother, a terrible person. My babies don't have me. But they're in good hands with Eric, and I'll be home soon. There'll be some tough times, some recrimination, some tears, maybe even some counseling with Pastor Ernie or some of the other do-gooder prudes at church. They'll tell me in their pinched little voices that they understand how a woman sometimes gets strange notions, that it's Satan speaking through me, that my weakness can lead to spiritual death and immortal damnation, blahblahblah....

"Fuck 'em," I say. I startle myself. My thoughts don't usually sneak out into words, especially profanity. Sometimes I'll cuss around Scooter, but that's just for a cheap thrill. Talking to myself, well, I must be getting addle-minded.

Handsome Jimmy turns and smiles. "Didn't think a bible-lovin' lady like you used that kind of language."

"I usually just think it."

He bats those long eyelashes at me and I feel something. Oh God. This guy, this...probable ex-con and who-knows-what-else, he's flirting with me and

I'm letting it hit, letting it penetrate my old married Christian mother's hide. My first thought is that I'm damned to hell for eternity, and my second thought is I like this a lot.

A lot.

Eric who?

Kids?

So this is how it happens. A good-looking stranger throws you a flirty grin and the next thing you know you're deserting your family, your life, your God.

I had toyed with the idea of hooking up somehow with Scooter, but now, suddenly, that's a distant, faint memory.

Scooter who?

I follow Handsome Jimmy down the road, and my hangover is gone. I feel good. Real good.

When we finally get back to the main highway I'm relieved to see that the minivan is still there. A piece of paper flaps under the wiper and I pull it out. It's a signed note from a cop saying *Your husband is looking for you. Call him.* I guess Eric figured out where I was headed and called the local cops to track me down.

"Nothing they can do about it," Handsome Jimmy says after he reads it. "You haven't done anything wrong."

"Yet."

He gives me that smile and eyelash bat again and my knees feel funny.

"Yet," he repeats. "Headin' home now?"

I unlock the minivan and sit down in the driver's seat. Pull the keys out of my fanny pack. Put them in the ignition. Start the engine. Look up at Handsome Jimmy.

Those eyelashes....

"Need a ride?" I ask.

"Sure."

"Where's your car?"

"Don't have one. I hitched up here."

"Uh-huh." I don't believe him. There's something he's not telling. Part of his appeal. The mystery.

"Climb in. Bet you've never ridden in a minivan before."

He hops in and we're driving.

Only I'm not headed home.

The gas station minimart is surrounded by cop cars, lights flashing blue and red and scary. Cop cars and everything about them scares me. Always has. Big guys with jangly belts, massive guns hanging on their hips, the noisy radios, the overwhelming sense that they're the authority and you better do what they say.

I don't know why I'm so paranoid about them; it's not like I've ever been arrested or anything. I dunno. Must be the religious guilt I'm filled with.

"Whataya suppose is goin' on here?" Handsome Jimmy asks. We've been driving through the desert for the last few hours not saying much. I'm not sure where we're headed. I'm sort of heading in the direction of home, but not really. Handsome Jimmy wondered if I'd take him on down Highway 87 a ways. He said he had a feeling this was the direction that Adonna and Randy and Scooter might be headed.

He didn't say why he thought that.

I'm slowing as we pass the crime scene gas station, nervous that one of the cops will recognize the minivan from some long forgotten parking ticket and before I know it I'll be in jail. Such guilt. That can't be healthy.

"Whatcha say we stop here. I'm kinda wondering what's goin' on. Gotta use the facilities anyway," Handsome Jimmy drawls. There's that vague southern accent again. I wonder where he's from? I'd ask, but he'd probably sidestep the question or lie.

"I don't think—"

"What's wrong? Johnny Law after you?" he teases.

I pull the minivan in to the side of the minimart. A couple of stern, spooky-looking state troopers eye us warily. I know what they're thinking: can't you morons see that there's trouble here and you're not gonna be able to buy a bag of Doritos and a Mountain Dew?

"I'll wait," I say.

"Okay."

He hops out and immediately starts chatting up the troopers. I watch him. He's got that easy masculinity, that one-of-the-boys ease that some men have...usually the jock guys. Eric used to be that way, before he got holy. Scooter never had it, even after all the years of writing about sports. He comes on too strong and needy almost...well, I hate to say it, but like a chick.

I giggle. Such thoughts.

Handsome Jimmys bullshits the troopers and before long he's waving "so long" and lopes off to the men's room. The troopers lean and chat. Others are inside the minimart busily doing whatever it is that cops do at crime scenes. These two guys outside are just holding up the wall. Maybe their job is to shoot the breeze with guys like Handsome Jimmy.

He wanders back over, gives the troopers another friendly wave, and gets in.

"Well?" I ask.

"Place got robbed."

"Those cops seem to like you."

"I got a way with the authorities," he smiles. "Had a lot of practice."

I don't pursue it. "What happened?"

Handsome Jimmy grins like he's heard the best joke in the world. "We should be gettin' along."

"What's so funny?"

"Start driving and I'll tell you. But I think we'd best get out of here."

I drive off, vaguely unsettled. We're on the road for five minutes, the featureless desert blurring by, before Handsome Jimmy starts talking, and he's still smiling.

"Guess who robbed the minimart?"

"Anybody I know?" I ask, being smart-alecky.

"Yep."

"I don't know anybody who'd—"

"Adonna. And your friend."

My mouth moves but I can't make sound come out.

"Funny, huh? Didn't think your pal had it in him, did you?"

"How...do you know it was them?" I finally croak like a raspy dying frog.

"Well, the description of Adonna's pretty vivid. She's hard to miss. And the guy the witnesses described who was with her sure wasn't Randy. They said he was kind of a wimpy-looking little dude with a receding hairline and that Adonna called him Scooter. Pretty sure that must be your Scooter. Haven't come across too many guys, at least grownups, who go by 'Scooter.' He needs to change that. If he ends up doing time in the joint that's not the kind of nickname you want." Handsome Jimmy laughs a full, throaty laugh, manly and very,

very amused.

"It's not funny!" I protest. "Scooter would never...."

"Seems like old Scoot's got in touch with his criminal side."

"Would Adonna hold up a minimart?"

"Sure. Probably isn't the first time."

"But she's a forest ranger!"

"So what? I didn't say robbery was her career, just a hobby." He laughs and laughs and I'm scared. I admit it. My walk on the wild side is turning out to be a little too wild.

"Have you?" I demand.

"What?"

"Robbed a store, a gas station, whatever."

"Done a lot of things. What matters is now, though. Not then."

"Oh great, I'm in a minivan in the middle of a desert with a...felon!"

"I'm not exactly sure if you're a felon forever. I think once you done your time and get off parole you're an ex-felon. Or maybe a former felon. Now your friend Scooter, he's a current felon."

"This isn't funny!"

"Look Erica, the world's full of all kinds of people. You've spent your life with one kind. That holy-roller husband of yours—"

"How do you know about him?!"

"You did a lot of talkin' last night."

Oh God. I'm afraid to ask what else I said. "Never mind him."

Handsome Jimmy sighs and stretches out. "What I'm sayin' is, in this world there's lots of different people doing different things. You've just been on one side of the fence. People like Adonna and me been on the other. And now it looks like old Scoot hopped over to our side."

"He wouldn't."

"He did."

"Maybe Adonna forced him. Or her husband."

"I doubt it. Neither one of them is real pushy."

"She robbed a minimart, for Christ's sake! I'd call that pushy!" I feel guilty using the Lord's name in vain, but this is a special case.

"Well, okay, I suppose you got me there. But she's only aggressive when she really needs to be. She probably needed some food or something."

"Has she ever heard of a Visa card?"

Handsome Jimmy chuckles. "You don't get it, do you?"

"Robbery? No."

"Sometimes you...well, not you personally, but people like me and Adonna...sometimes we do things just 'cause we can. Because we want to."

"Robbery? Holding guns at people's faces?! That's savagery."

Handsome Jimmy sighs like I'm the biggest moron in the world. "If that's what you think...you gotta understand the excitement."

"In crime?"

"Yeah."

"But you hurt innocent people."

"I don't hurt people. Ever," Handsome Jimmy says coldly.

"But if you stick up a minimart you frighten innocent people, you take things that don't belong to you."

"They get over it. And whatever gets took belongs to big companies.

Who gives a shit about big companies?"

"I can't believe we're having this conversation. People own big companies, and you don't take what doesn't belong to you."

"I think of it more as sharing. Rich giving to the poor, you know? All that religious stuff you and your hubby are into says that, doesn't it? Help out the poor, donate what extra you have."

"That's different."

"Not really. It's just that instead of waitin' for it to be donated, sometimes people like me and Randy and Adonna take it. We just speed up the process."

I look over at Handsome Jimmy. He's looking at me so seriously, like he's just made an incredibly deep philosophical point, that I can't help but laugh. "You're amazing. You really believe it, don't you?"

"Sure," he says, batting those eyelashes at me. He uses them like weapons.

I don't know what else to say. This guy is a charming sociopath. It's time to....

What's it time to do? I don't know.

"Where are we headed?" I ask.

"Where you want to go?"

"I don't know. Home. No, not home. Yeah, home. I should go home to my kids."

"Yeah. Kids need their mom, I suppose."

"I should find Scooter. He might need me."

"Maybe. You in love with this guy?"

"No. Once. Maybe. I don't know."

"You're saying 'I don't know' a lot."

"I don't know what to do."

"Your choice. You're free."

Free. What a delicious word. I am free. Free to go home to Eric and the kids. Free to go find Scooter and save him. Free to do...whatever.

"What do you think I should I do, Jimmy?" I ask quietly.

"Not my call. But I know what I'd do if I was in your shoes, though."

"What?"

Handsome Jimmy looks at me and I look at him. He gives me his killer smile, and bats those eyelashes, and I know instantly with utter clarity what I'm going to do.

Chapter Ten

Betrayal and abandonment is so much easier once you get used to the idea.

Maybe it's because you can always rationalize doing bad things. Pastor Ernie thunders on and on about rationalization, how it's Satan's reasoning, how it can spin you into a sin spiral that you'll never escape from. I think he's even likened it to the vortex of a toilet. Pretty grim, but then, he's a plumber, so how else would a plumber explain the nature of sin? It paints a mental picture that has always stuck with me.

And right now, at this minute, I'm swirling, being sucked down into the depths of Satan's sewer.

And I can't make myself care. Or stop.

I...feel good about being a wild thing.

Not that I'm doing anything that wild at the moment.

I'm sitting in a dumpy room in a Motel 6 in a dumpy desert town. We'd been driving forever after we left the scene of Scooter's crime—I still couldn't get used to *that* idea—when we finally rolled the dusty minivan into Grubbs. Great name for a town. Better than something false, I suppose, like Pleasantville or Rose City. But Grubbs. *Blech.* Probably named after some long-dead miner, but all I could think of were white fleshy little wiggling blobs of bug babies, and it made me want to throw up.

Handsome Jimmy insisted on taking me out to dinner at a dirty little Mexican restaurant. He even paid.

"Is it stolen?" I asked when he offered to pay for my lard-filled enchiladas. Which isn't to say they weren't great.

Handsome Jimmy flashed me a grin. "What difference does it make?" he asked. "As long as you eat."

I didn't complain. Arguing ethics with him was a lost cause.

We had a couple of Tecates before dinner. After last night's drunk fest I didn't think I'd ever drink again, but the beer tasted good. It made me mad I'd gone so long without even having the occasional nip of something. All the religious stuff had kept me from a lot of pleasure. I found myself being angry at Eric. I didn't have the guts to admit that I was the problem. I let myself be pushed around.

"Are you ever going to tell me what you've done?" I asked over the beers.

"Done?"

"Crime wise."

"The usual. Mass murder. Nothing special."

"Be serious."

"How do you know I'm not?"

"Because. You're not the murdering type. You said you don't hurt people."

Handsome Jimmy drained his beer and ordered another. "Coulda been lying. You never know. I mighta been the guy behind the grassy knoll."

"Except you weren't born yet."

"I've aged well."

I couldn't help myself. I liked this guy. We're from about as far apart as two people can get, but beneath his criminal exterior was a droll, witty guy with more than just a hint of intelligence. I think he just likes to hide it behind his jailbird façade.

"Do you work?" I asked.

"When I have to."

"What do you do?"

"Whatever. Construction. Been a bouncer in a biker bar. Drove trucks. Roofer. You name it. Jack of all trades, master of one."

"Which one?"

He grinned but said nothing.

"Okay," I pressed on. I'd spent enough time with Handsome Jimmy to feel like I could interrogate him. He'd clam up if he didn't want to answer anyway, or lie. But that was okay, lies were interesting, too. "How about wives?"

"Couple ex's."

"Kids?"

For the first time since we'd hooked up, those cold eyes looked a little wistful. "One."

"Boy or girl?"

"Girl. She's in high school." He reached for his wallet, and I thought he might get a picture out for me, but then he decided against it and leaned his elbows on the table.

"What's her name?"

"Tish," he said in a low voice.

"You see her?"

"Nope. Her mother doesn't care much for me."

I felt a sudden stab of regret. Sad for Handsome Jimmy that he was estranged from his daughter, and sad for me that I'd left my own brood. But I'd be back in the nest soon enough; I'd decided that this road trip would only last a few more days. Just long enough to rescue Scooter, then I'd go back. To what, I wasn't entirely sure. Eric would forgive, but I don't know if I could forget. My tiny little pathetic taste of freedom was too intoxicating to forget—and too intoxicating not to try again.

I tried to pump Handsome Jimmy some more, but I guess bringing up his daughter made him sad, and he wouldn't talk much after that. He seemed distracted.

He slept in the minivan—he said he was a little short on cash and I sure wasn't going to invite him into my room. I may have been on Mr. Toad's Wild Ride, but sharing my room...well, that wasn't in the cards.

Yet.

And now I'm sitting alone, staring at the horrible, mass-produced clipper ship painting hanging crookedly over the fake wood dresser, debating whether to turn on the TV and stare at CNN or the Weather Channel. Sometimes at home Eric and I watch the Weather Channel for an hour at a time. It's freaky, but we find it compelling. Watching the swirling cloud patterns and weather systems, the perky weathercasters explaining it all with such precision and certainty—even though in our part of the world what they say is usually wrong. I grab the remote and click on the TV. The cable must only half work, because everything is fuzzy and the sound warbly. But I luck out and find the Weather Channel and for a few minutes all is right with the world as I watch cutoff lows and ridging highs. I almost forget that I'm away from home and Scooter held up a minimart and I'm alone in a dumpy motel in the middle of nowhere and there's a stranger sleeping out in my minivan.

I guess I'm not surprised to find the minivan and Handsome Jimmy gone in the morning.

I fell asleep to the Weather Channel, and dreamed of storm fronts and "Coming right up, the Western Forecast!" When I awakened different weather-casters were talking about new weather, it was light outside, and for some reason I felt great. Maybe sleeping with the Weather Channel on was the answer to serenity.

After the morning body maintenance chores I went outside to see what Handsome Jimmy was up to.

And that's when I found that he and the minivan were gone.

I waited around, wanting to give him the benefit of the doubt. He went to the grocery store, went to pick up some Wheaties or yogurt or...rob someplace.

Oh great. He'll knock over a liquor store and I'll get blamed because some bystander will scribble down the license plate number. I worry about that for a good fifteen minutes until I convince myself that's the least of my problems, then I decide to go into the motel's lobby to inquire about Handsome Jimmy—and make sure I have an alibi witness.

A hard-looking woman with dark roots and smoker's skin is watching a video on MTV with half-naked girls gyrating around a thuggish, pierced-all-over-the-place guy. It surprises me. The desk clerk looks like she should be watching *Judge Judy* or country music videos.

"Help you?" she asks, not taking her eyes off the TV.

"Have you seen...." I'm not sure how to describe him.

"Good-looking guy you come in with?"

"Yeah."

"He left a couple hours ago."

Wonderful. "He didn't happen to say where he was going, did he?"

The woman gives me a long, annoyed look. "I just saw him get in the minivan and drive off. We didn't visit."

I slink outside, knowing that the dark-rooted desk clerk thinks I got dumped by a quickie lover. I don't know why I care what she thinks, but I do. It bothers me. I suppose I hate to be thought of as dumpable.

I go back to my room. What now? I guess I should call the police and report the minivan stolen, but for some reason I can't make myself do it. I can't rat out Handsome Jimmy. He's taken advantage of me, stolen something that's mine, yet I still can't make myself turn him in.

Why?

I could call Eric to come get me. That's a horrible option. I'd have to face a long drive filled with recriminations and bible preaching and things I'm not ready to face.

I sit on the bed for hours, not moving, not doing anything.

I don't know what I think will happen, but I expect something...big, so I sit on the bed and wait. I watch the Weather Channel. Some of the men weathercasters are really quite handsome; most of the women strike me as a little Barbie-dollish. Probably all the makeup they wear. But the interplay between the males and females is interesting. The men seem almost subservient to the women; there must be something in weather school, maybe secret initiation rites or some kind of matriarchal thing....

Jeez, what am I thinking? It's like I'm hallucinating. Endless hours of Weather Channel makes you start thinking crazy.

I'm pondering my new psychoses when there's knock on the door. At first I think it's on TV, because right at that moment the weathercaster is pointing at a swirling potential hurricane off the African coast, and, and....

Another knock. Definitely the door.

I stand, click off the TV. They probably want to clean the room, or the dark-rooted desk clerk is coming to tell me it's time to pay up for another night or clear out.

I open the door, expecting, well, I don't know.

So I'm surprised to see Handsome Jimmy standing there, a shy little smile tugging at the corners of his mouth.

"Hey," he says.

"Hi," I say.

"Probably didn't think you'd see me again, huh?"

"Nope."

"Yeah," he drawls, leaning against the doorjamb. "I didn't think I'd be back either."

I look out behind him into the parking lot. There's the minivan, safe and sound. "You didn't use it for a crime, did you?"

"Now there you go," he says, almost sounding insulted. "You shouldn't just expect the worst from people."

"But you stole the minivan, right?"

"Maybe. Not really. I dunno. But I brought it back."

"You still took it. And until...whatever reason brought you back, you were gonna keep it, weren't you?"

Handsome Jimmy stares down at his lizard skin boots. "Yeah. Probably."

"Why'd you come back?"

He makes a big production out of lighting a cigarette. I think that's the main reason people smoke, it's not really about the nicotine and addiction, it's more of something to fill the conversational gaps. It keeps them busy.

He finally finishes lighting it and inhales down into his toes. "I missed you," he says, and looks up with those damned eyelashes waving at me. But I'm not biting.

"Bullshit," I say, rather proud of myself for getting a reaction out of him. He almost takes a step back, like I punched him or spit on his boots.

"It's true!"

"No it's not. You came back because you want something else, or maybe you felt guilty about leaving me stranded, although I'm not sure that you're capable of guilt. But you sure didn't come back because you missed me."

He shrugs and then grins at me. "Decided I'm not a minivan kind of guy."

I grab my suitcase, click off the Weather Channel, pay the dark-rooted desk clerk who's more interested in doing a barfly flirt thing with Handsome Jimmy rather than running my credit card—and then before I know it we're back on the road.

"So where are we going?" I ask a few hours later as we click off endless miles of desert highway. "I'm going back to my husband and my kids," I add with something less than enthusiasm. But the guilt gets me anyway. I wonder how little Eli's doing?

"I got an idea where they might be headed."

"Where is it?"

"A ways."

"Where?"

The firm, kid-scolding tone in my voice must've gotten his attention, because he immediately answers, "New Mexico."

"How far is New Mexico?" I ask, not entirely sure what state we're in right now.

"A ways."

"Why would they be going there?"

Handsome Jimmy stretches out. He adjusts the seat back as far as it will go, but his boots still stick up underneath the dark reaches of the dashboard. It's so strange to be driving with somebody other than kids or Eric. It reminds me again how sheltered I've become. How many normal people would even think about the excitement of somebody new in the passenger seat?

"We've done business there before. It's a good place to hang."

"After you've robbed a minimart?"

"Something like that," he grins. "You oughta lighten up on me, Erica. I'm not really so bad. Now Adonna, she's another story."

"How bad is she?" I ask, and I don't know why, but I get a cold, tingly sensation of fear. It takes me a second to realize I'm afraid for Scooter.

"The thing you have to understand about Adonna," Handsome Jimmy says, lighting another of his endless cigarettes—he's on the way to emphysema—"is that she's had a tough life. And a tough life can make you hard."

"She was just an ordinary kid in high school. What happened to her?"

"Life."

"Life happened to me, too. And I'm not...bad."

"You're religious. Same thing." He says it with that irresistible grin and eyelash bat.

"What happened to her?"

He exhales a big cloud of Marlboro into the minivan. Eric's going to go nuts. He'll never get the smell out of the upholstery. It'll smell like those nasty rental cars you get that are supposedly "smoke-free" but always stink like ash-trays anyway.

"She made some mistakes."

"Like what? Is this twenty questions?"

"Well, first off she married me," Handsome Jimmy says. Wistfully.

"Really?"

"Yeah. She was my second wife. Met her in...where was it? Must've been a tavern up in Spokane."

"So tell me the story."

"Not much to tell. I was up there workin' on a new hotel, pouring concrete, bumped into her one night after work, had some beers, hooked up."

"That's so romantic."

Handsome Jimmy smiles. "I left out the romantic part. Being that you're religious and all. I could go into it, if you'd like."

I don't know why I do it, I'm going to fry in hell, but I say, "Tell me."

Handsome Jimmy shakes his head, takes a deep draw on his Marlboro. "You gotta let go of that religion stuff. Makes a woman strange."

"Tell me," I say, and my voice is husky, whispery. I want to know exactly what happened.

He smiles, hesitates, then nods. "Okay. Adonna probably wouldn't like me tellin', but seein' as she isn't here, what the hell?"

"Never mind, I don't want to know," I blurt. What was I thinking?

"Too late. So I'm drinkin' after a long day's work, and I see this sorta hot woman. She's alone at a booth, and boy, I'll tell you, she looked good to me.

Nice rack, and even though she was sittin' I got the feeling she had a good ass." Handsome Jimmy grins at me, enjoying being crude. "Want me to go on?"

"No! I already told you, I changed my mind."

"I think I'll go on anyway. Do you good to hear what goes on in a man's mind. Hate to break it to you, but even that bible-thumper husband of yours looks at women the same way."

"Eric doesn't think like a normal guy," I say, buzzy at the secret thrill of dissing my husband. What's wrong with me?

"If he's got a set of balls, I guarantee you he thinks the same way we all think. Can't help ourselves from being pigs. Some of us are just more honest about it, that's all."

I look over at Handsome Jimmy. I can't read his face. I'm usually pretty good at sizing people up, but this guy absolutely confounds me.

"So I go over to her booth. 'Buy you a drink?' I ask. 'Sure,' she says. And she looks me right in the eye, real direct. I like that in a woman. No fake shit, none of that flirty bullshit. She was just straight up. Kinda reminds me of you, to be honest with you."

I feel my face blushing red hot. "You don't need to tell me this, okay?"

"So I sit down," he continues, "and we start talkin'. She's in Spokane because she followed some asshole up there she thought she was in love with, then the fool drops her, so she's stuck. Worked as a bookkeeper...she's pretty smart, you know." Handsome Jimmy sighs, apparently warmed by the memory of his first meeting with Adonna. It's kind of nice, really. Okay, they met in a bar, but at least—

"So when she reached over and unzipped my pants I was kinda shocked, to tell you the truth."

"She did that? It's so...gross!"

"Well, it's not like it was bad or anything, just unexpected. We'd only been talking for a little while, but I 'spose it's my irresistible ways that got to her."

"At least you're humble."

"I'm kiddin', Erica. Jesus, don't be so literal."

I resist the urge to be a smart-ass and ask him if he even knows what literal means. I need to work on my superiority complex...it's not like I deserve one.

"Is this a fantasy, then?"

"No, the unzipping part is real. Just the irresistible part. I made that up. 'Course, from a man's point of view, when a woman unzips him, she must be feelin' that he's somewhat irresistible."

"I wouldn't know. Please stop. This is none of my business."

"You're right about that. But I feel like talking. Think of it as a letter to Penthouse being read aloud to you."

I should keep demanding that he stop, but I don't.

Because, in spite of myself, in spite of my better nature, I want to hear the rest of the story. It's that old forbidden fruit thing again.

"So anyway," he says, "Adonna does some serious hand-jobbing under the table. And I'm pretty riled up, to be truthful. Been around a lot of women, but something about Adonna...."

"What about her? Other than the fact that she commits sex felonies in public?"

"She...she's got this power. Hard to explain. It's like she's stronger than a guy, but she looks like a hot chick. That make sense?"

"Sounds to me like you've got issues."

"Yeah. They say we've all got a little faggot in us."

"Is that out of a book?"

"I paraphrased," Handsome Jimmy says. He's not just a good-looking scoundrel—he's got a brain rattling around up there behind those beautiful eyes. He's just lacking a conscience and class.

"You're losing focus. What happened next?"

"Thought you didn't want to hear it?"

"I want to get it over with."

"Well," he says, smug that he's got my attention with his smutty story. "Adonna works me over pretty good, so then, right at kind of a critical moment, she invites me to her place. Takes me awhile to get everything in order, but I finally follow her over to her apartment. It's a junky little place downtown. Ever been to Spokane? Not a place you really want to spend a lot of time at. Anyway, by the time I get to her door, I'm, well, ready. And so's she." Handsome Jimmy lights a new Marlboro from the old. "How much detail you want?"

"Just tell the story."

"Okay. We get inside, close the door, and the clothes start flying. She's got my pants around my ankles before I can say 'Howdy'. And then she's...you know."

"What?" I ask. I know what he's talking about, but for some perverted reason I want to hear it.

"Well," he says, and he actually sounds embarrassed. "She's sucking me."

"And what did you do for her?"

"Huh?"

"She blows you, what did you do for her?"

"Well, later, we screwed."

"That's it? Why didn't you return the favor?"

"You mean go down on her?"

"Yeah."

"I dunno. I did after we'd been together for awhile. You gotta understand, Adonna was kind of a wild woman. Kissing her was like sucking cock by proxy, I didn't even want to think about going down on her until I knew her for awhile."

"That's so...lame. It's selfish."

"She didn't seem to mind."

I don't bother arguing with him. I haven't had much experience with that kind of sleazy sex, but plain old fairness says he should've returned the favor to Adonna right then and there.

"So she blows you, then what?"

Handsome Jimmy shakes his head. The desert scenery whips by unseen by me; I'm in that scuzzy little apartment in Spokane with Jimmy and Adonna. I want to know what happens next.

"Man, you religious women...that husband of yours ever take care of your needs?"

"This is your story, not mine."

"Okay, okay. So we start havin' a lot of really good sex—which, of course, leads us to gettin' married."

"Of course."

"Hey, maybe we didn't meet at bible study, but at least we sorta cared about each other."

"When you were naked."

"Mostly," he agrees. "But even when we had clothes on we were fond of one another."

"So then what?"

"We stayed up there till my job ran out. That's when the trouble started."

"What kind of trouble?"

"Well...."

Handsome Jimmy stares out the window. The air conditioner is blowing tepid. I'll have to have Eric take a look at it when I get home. *If* I get home. What am I thinking?

"We got into some bad things. Met some bad people. Lived some bad ways."

"Drugs?"

"Yep."

"What kind?"

"The usual. The thing that got us, though, was the crank."

"Meth?"

"Good old meth-am-pheta-*mine*. It's weird. Even now I want it bad. Word makes me feel good just to hear it. Scares the shit outa me, too."

"Do you still....?"

"Nope. Shit'll kill you. Almost killed Adonna. That's what happened to her face."

I look over at him. I guess the question on *my* face is obvious.

"She and Randy were cooking up a batch—we were sellin' at the time—but the shit blew up. It's kinda dangerous."

"What happened to her face?"

"Got all fucked up. Scars and shit. She kinda looks like a monster on one side. Still pretty on the other, though."

"Is that why you divorced her?"

"Now see, there you go, makin' judgments about me. I loved Adonna. She just had some trouble afterwards, wanted to get away from everybody she knew. That's how she ended up at the ghost town."

Wow. Adonna a disfigured, drug-peddling-sex-crazed-addict-thief—What did I get Scooter into?

"Who's Randy?"

"A friend. Used to be a friend, anyway. Now he's...just a dirtbag. Still mixes up shit last I heard."

"Why were you going to Skull Peak?"

Handsome Jimmy sighs. Sadly. The twinkly jokey eyes are serious.

"I thought I might...get Adonna back."

"Really?" Maybe I've misjudged old Handsome Jimmy.

"Heard through the grapevine that Randy was gonna hook up with her. She never could resist the motherfucker. I knew if he was going to the fuckin' ghost town he was gonna be up to no good. What I didn't expect was that she'd hit the road with your boyfriend."

"Scooter's not my boyfriend."

Handsome Jimmy snorts derisively. "Whatever you say, Erica."

"He's not."

"Ain't saying you're gonna blow him. I'm just sayin' that you've got unfinished business with the guy. I got perception about stuff like this. You know, affairs of the heart."

"You've read too many romance novels," I say coldly.

"I buy 'em for the covers," he grins.

"Scooter's just...a really good friend. We were band fags."

He looks at me questioningly and I explain the whole Scooter/Erica boring life story. By the time I'm finished I can't tell whether he's about to fall asleep or incredibly interested or—

"Sounds to me," he says in that slow drawl, "like you married the wrong guy."

"I don't—"

"See, the thing is, when you had your little drinking session, you badmouthed your husband like he was the biggest asshole in the world. Religious, good guy, but an asshole. 'A boring bible-humper.' Your words, not mine."

"I said that?"

"Yep. Said you loved your kids, but the old man, well, that was another story."

"I was drunk."

"It's been my experience that people usually tell the truth when they're shit-faced. Might be a sloppy truth, but it's truth now matter how you slice it."

Bible-humper? That's so sacrilegious. I start to giggle.

"What?" Handsome Jimmy asks.

"Nothing." But I can't help laughing. Pretty soon tears are rolling down my cheeks. Handsome Jimmy just shakes his head.

"You're one weird chick."

Another minimart surrounded by cop cars.

Handsome Jimmy grins as we pull up. "Sumbitch. Adonna and Scooter been busy, looks to me."

"You don't know for sure it was them," I say, knowing for sure it *was* them. "Out here there's got to be lots of minimart-robbing lowlifes."

"Yep. People like me."

"Sure."

"Or people like Adonna and Scooter. Comin' in?"

This time I get out of the minivan and follow Handsome Jimmy inside.

The store is still open for business, and the tired and cranky-looking old guy who runs it is trying to sell Slim Jims and cigarettes while a bunch of scary state troopers surround the video monitor and replay the robbery.

"Marlboros," Handsome Jimmy drawls. "And a five buck lotto quick pick."

"You feel lucky?" I ask.

"Met you, didn't I?"

My face glows red-hot while the grubby clerk tosses the Marlboros on the counter.

"Cash or annuity?" the old guy asks. His face is pocked and his nose is bulbous and angry red. He's going to look like W.C. Fields in a few years.

"Cash," Handsome Jimmy says. "Ain't it something how you gotta pretend to do financial planning when you buy a lotto ticket nowadays?" Handsome Jimmy says to nobody in particular. The cops rerun and rerun the tape, and I edge closer to get a peek at the tiny little monitor.

"It's Scarface," one of the cops says. Handsome Jimmy's head pivots toward the cops. I feel the blood drain out of my face, run through my guts, and pool in my feet. *Oh god.* Adonna.

"Can't get a look at the guy," another cop says. "Kinda nondescript. But the woman. No way she can blend in."

Handsome Jimmy pays W.C. "Get held up, did you?" he asks.

"Some freak with a messed up face and her boyfriend."

I watch Handsome Jimmy's jaw clench at the word "freak".

"Did they have a gun?" I ask stupidly. When one of the cops looks over at me with a curious glance I get scared. I'm terrified of authority figures. Probably from all the hellfire and damnation that's been jammed down my throat all these years.

The old guy grumbles and shuffles off. If he answered me, it wasn't in any language I've ever heard.

The cop who looked over at me hasn't stopped studying me. He looks at Handsome Jimmy, too. Then, to my horror, he walks over to us.

"How you doin'?" Handsome Jimmy asks. There's that easy grin. I wish I could do that.

"How are you folks today?" the cop asks. He couldn't be more than twenty-five. Babyface. But he's carrying a gun, so he still scares me.

"Just fine, officer. Funny, we stopped at another minimart a ways back and damned if it hadn't just been robbed. Got an epidemic goin' out here, huh?"

Babyface nods and looks us over. Actually, he looks Jimmy over. And as I study Handsome Jimmy, I can see why. He's got jailbird written all over him. It's not that he has wall-to-wall swastika tattoos, or the just-out-of-the-joint look that you see on ex-cons in movies and TV, but still.... Maybe it's the arrogance, the defiance of authority that stands out. Handsome Jimmy has somehow gotten bigger, like he's puffed out in the presence of the law.

There's something outlaw about Handsome Jimmy. And even Babyface the cop can see it.

"Do I know you?" Babyface asks. He's fishing, I can tell.

"Don't believe so," Handsome Jimmy grins. "I don't know many cops. Socially, at least."

And when Babyface cop glances at me, I look away. Guiltily. But he doesn't do anything, just turns and goes back to his comrades studying the video.

"Have a nice day, Officer," Handsome Jimmy grins.

"Let's get out of here," I whisper. The old guy behind the counter is looking strangely at me, and I feel the hot shame of guilt—except I don't know what I feel guilty about.

When we get back in the minivan, Handsome Jimmy's laughing at me.

"Slick. Real slick."

"I wasn't cut out to be a criminal."

"Didn't realize going into a minimart to buy cigs was a crime."

"You know what I mean!"

"Jesus Christ, Erica, you're gonna explode feelin' guilty about nothing all the time. Is that what you learn at your little church? Sneak around like the world's gonna kick you in the balls?"

"You don't understand. You don't have a conscience."

I climb into the minivan. Handsome Jimmy stands at the passenger door. He looks in at me, and I can't tell if he's getting ready to throw me one of those grins or—

"Fuck you, honey," he says. He slams the passenger door and strides away. I sit, not sure what to do next. I don't owe this guy anything, he's a crazy criminal, I shouldn't be out here with him anyway, it's time to go home to Eric and the kids, I should start the minivan and drive away and forget about Handsome Jimmy and all this.

But I don't.

I sit and watch.

Handsome Jimmy walks alongside the road, casually hanging his thumb out as cars and trucks roar by. By the slouchy body language I can tell he's hitched many times before.

And as I watch him, I'm suddenly hit with pity for the guy. He's had a rough time, sure, some of it's been his own doing, but still, he deserves a break. He's out here trying to track down the woman he loves, and I'm making it harder for him. Maybe he wants to rescue her, maybe he wants to try and put her on the straight and narrow path.

Well, maybe not straight and narrow, but at least something better than crank and holding up minimarts.

I really should stay with him, at least until we find Scooter and Adonna. I owe it to him. And I owe it to Scooter.

When I pull out to the highway I've got two choices: right or left. Home or Handsome Jimmy and the unknown.

It's a surprisingly easy choice.

Chapter Eleven

"The thing about you, Erica," Handsome Jimmy is saying as we cross the border into New Mexico, "is that you've never really lived. Been a cute little hausfrau breeder since you were still a kid, you never seen how the rest of the world is."

I'm fixated on the word "cute" for a moment before I can respond. Handsome Jimmy's driving now. I know I shouldn't let him, but I was tired of driving and anyway, I trust him.

Sort of.

Well, maybe trust is too strong of a word. I don't...fear him quite so much.

"Everybody goes down different paths," I point out, calmly and coolly. I think Pastor Ernie said that in a sermon once. But now that I think of it, he was talking about people taking the wrong path and how there's only one right path, the path of righteousness and Jesus.

Anyway, Handsome Jimmy doesn't need to know that. It was a cool, zen master response.

"That's a horseshit answer, it doesn't mean anything," Handsome Jimmy says.

And here I thought I sounded so cool. "Not everybody can be a criminal," I say. I sound snarky and petulant. I wish I was slicker.

"That's not what I'm sayin'," he says. "What I'm sayin' is that people like you don't live. They...exist."

"Yeah, yeah, yeah, and people like you and Adonna and her druggie ex-husband, you're the real people. The ones who rob minimarts and really live life to its fullest. Talk about horseshit."

Handsome Jimmy smiles, then laughs.

"What?" I ask.

"It's funny to hear you cuss."

"Now you're just making fun of me."

"No. It's kinda...cute."

There's that word again. "Cute". Has Eric ever said I was cute? Scooter might've once, I can't remember. But Eric, never.

I savor the cute moment, but then I realize I need to argue. He's dead wrong.

"What if everybody was like you guys? There wouldn't be any minimarts to rob."

"Yeah, maybe. You got a point, I guess."

"And cops. There wouldn't be any of them if the world was wall-to-wall take whatever you want kinda people."

"No great loss, if you ask me."

"Don't you ever feel...wrong?"

"Sure."

"When?"

"Taking your minivan. That didn't seem right."

"See!" I say. "You do have a conscience."

Handsome Jimmy sighs. "Don't tell nobody."

"Ruin your image?"

Handsome Jimmy just smiles. I'm tempted to press the conversation, but why beat it to death? He knows I'm right, and any more chatter is just that.

"Are you sure they'll be where we're going?" I ask, changing the subject.

"Pretty sure. Adonna's a creature of habit. Randy too, when he's not fucked up."

"How come," I ask, "they'd let Scooter come along with them?"

"I was wondering that myself. Randy's not the socialest guy in the world. Especially if he knew your Scoot friend was lookin' to hook up with Adonna. Randy's kinda possessive that way."

"They must be forcing him."

"Maybe."

"Like when Patty Hearst robbed those banks, they brainwashed her and forced her to do it."

"Don't think Randy's the brainwashin' type. He might threaten to kill you, but he don't have enough brains of his own to wash, let alone somebody else's."

"Poor Scooter," I say, suddenly filled with dread. My buddy, my pal, I put him up to this and now he's in trouble. "We have to find him," I say.

Handsome Jimmy looks over at me. I can't get over that somebody besides Eric is in the driver's seat.

"We'll find 'em, Erica," Handsome Jimmy says tenderly. "I promise you."

The long eyelashes melt me. If I wasn't married and a godly woman and he wasn't a felon I'd kiss him.

We roll to a stop on a county road. I've never been in this kind of country before. It's scrubby desert, but with pinyon pines and weathered buttes it has its own solitary beauty. I roll down the window. The air is deliciously dry, sweet with the juniper odor of the pines and the musky scent of the desert soil.

"It's pretty here," I say to Handsome Jimmy. His eyes are fixed, staring off into the distance. I can't see what he's looking at.

"Yeah," he says, not looking at me. "Nice country if you like the great outdoors."

"Which I take it you don't."

Handsome Jimmy turns and smiles at me. "I grew up in a place a lot like this...don't hold much fascination for me."

"Are they nearby?"

"Yeah. I think so."

"Then why don't we go see them?"

Handsome Jimmy fires up a new Marlboro. He's gone five minutes without one, and I was wondering how long he'd last.

"I'm not all that sure how welcome we're gonna be, Erica."

When he says my name it give me a...cheap thrill. I don't know why.

"When Scooter sees my minivan pull up, he'll be glad."

"It ain't Scoot I'm worried about."

"I thought they were your friends?"

"You never can tell with people," Handsome Jimmy drawls. I suppose he's right. Drug-addled thieves probably tend to be a little flaky where friendship is concerned.

"I think Randy's a little unsure 'bout me and Adonna. Like we got unfinished business or something."

"Do you?"

He doesn't answer.

"Since you came looking for her and all, I mean," I say. "Seems like maybe you—"

"Drop it, Erica."

Ooo-kay. His friendly, long-lashed aw-shucks demeanor evaporates in a hurry when he's annoyed. I don't know him well enough to push it.

"So how long do we sit here? Is it gonna be a commando raid, or do we drive right up?"

"I think," he says with a sigh, "that we drive right up and hope for the best. This friend of yours will recognize this rig, right?"

"Sure."

"I hope so. 'Cause if he doesn't, and they get twitchy, no way to tell what Randy and Adonna might do."

He turns the key and off we go.

We turn off the main road and bounce along a rutted trail, a pair of dirt ribbons stretching through the sage. I'm tempted to tell Handsome Jimmy to take it easy, it *is* a minivan after all, but I don't say anything. Part of my new, daring self.

It's just going to be hard to explain to Eric why the underside of the van is all beat up. Oh well, probably time to trade it in anyway.

We bounce along for a couple of miles, and the road, such as it is, gets rougher. Scrubby brush scratches against the van's side. There goes the paint job.

"How much further?" I ask, sounding like one of the kids. It always drives me nuts when they badger us about "When are we gonna get there?" in their whiny little voices. I doubt it sounds much better coming from me.

Handsome Jimmy says nothing. There's no reason to, because we pull up in front of a shabby-looking old ranch house. It's backed up against a knobby mesa. Defensible, it seems. No way to sneak up on them.

"Doesn't look like anybody's here," I say.

"Uh-huh." Handsome Jimmy stares at the house. We're parked in a gravel turn-around by a broken-down corral. No sign of life anywhere. I'm convinced he's wrong. They couldn't possibly be here.

"Looks deserted, don't it, Erica?"

"Yeah."

"It ain't."

"How do you know?"

Handsome Jimmy nods toward the mesa behind the house. "Look up there. Stare real close at the opening by the dead tree."

I gaze at the spot. Just a dark space between rocks. By the dead tree. Way up on the orange rocks and....

"Ooooh..." I say. A movement. I saw it. Something—or someone—is moving.

"Yeah...they're up there."

"Are you sure it isn't a goat or something?"

Handsome Jimmy's not an eye-rolling kind of guy, but if he was, now would be the time. "They ain't shot at us yet, so that's a good sign, I suppose." He opens the door. Tentatively.

"Are you sure this is such a good idea?" I ask, suddenly worried.

"We'll find out."

He steps out of the van and stands up straight. I half expect gunshots.

"ERICA? RANDY? SCOOT? You up there? It's me."

A woman's voice—I assume it's Adonna—echoes down from above. "What're *you* doing here?"

"Come to make sure you're okay. Where's Randy?"

"Dead."

Handsome Jimmy peers back in at me. "That's a relief," he says quietly. Then, shouting up to Adonna, "What happened to him?"

"Scooter shot him."

I'm glad I'm not standing, because I probably would've fainted. Handsome Jimmy looks in at me. "That seem likely?" he asks.

"I...I...don't think so. But then, I didn't think he'd rob minimarts, either."

"Huh," Handsome Jimmy says, thoroughly perplexed. I sense a new respect for Scooter.

"C'mon down, Adonna. It's just me and Scoot's old girlfriend Erica."

"ERICA!" Scooter's voice yells out, shocked and amazed. "WHY ARE YOU HERE?"

I get out of the minivan and shout back up at the mesa. I still can't see them. "WHY ARE *YOU*?!"

"ASKED YOU FIRST!" he says, giggling. He sounds weird, like he's wired or something.

"Ol' Scoot do drugs?" Handsome Jimmy asks. He obviously heard it, too.

"No. At least not in the past. Now, who knows?"

We watch as Adonna and Scooter scramble down the hillside toward us. I'm scared now. I don't know what to expect.

"And then I got hit by lightning!" Scooter says with a huge, happy grin. He's giggling again, like he's on coke or speed or...maybe he's just glad to see me. It's the weirdest thing, it's like I don't know him anymore. He's only been gone a few days, but whatever happened to him has completely changed him. I can't imagine the vaguely nerdy sports reporter with the bitchy wife and crabby kid that he was three weeks ago. Now he's a lightning-struck, convenience-store-robbing, Randy-shooting stranger.

Oh God, please forgive me. This was all my idea.

We're sitting in the, I guess you'd call it the living room, of the old ranch house. The place is a smelly dive. It might've been nice once, and could be again, but it'd need a major Martha Stewart clean up and revival. Now, it's just beat and worn and has the air of a hideout.

Handsome Jimmy's smoking another Marlboro. Adonna bummed one off of him and there's been continuous smoke since we arrived. I can't look at Adonna, but I can't *not* look at her, either. Her face is hideous. Why doesn't she get surgery, or wear a scarf or...something? I know it's not Christian, but I'm not sure I qualify as a Christian anymore, so what the fuck, I'll think what I like.

I stifle a giggle. There I go again. Walking on the wild side, being irreligious. Eric will never get me back to church, that's for sure. He may want to divorce me when he hears me start talking again. Who knows? But there I go again, my mind's wandering. Got to watch that.

Adonna is surly and unpleasant. She looks at me like I'm some kind of enemy who's going to call the cops and turn her in. I don't really care enough about her to do anything at this point. I just want Scooter back.

Scooter.

What in the world has come over him?

"Pretty cool, huh Er?" he's saying. I wasn't focused on what came before, so I haven't the faintest idea what he's talking about. Handsome Jimmy and Adonna are off to the corner mumbling seriously to each other in clouds of Marlboro smoke. Me and Scooter sit on the sprung floral couch. He's jittery and wired, hyper. Weird.

"Have you been doing drugs?" I ask.

"Nope. Wouldn't touch that stuff," he says with an odd giggle at the end of the sentence. He sure sounds druggie to me.

"Then what on earth is wrong with you?"

Scooter scoots closer to me, drapes his arm around my shoulder. We've been pals forever, but have never done much touchy-feely stuff. He's too close, it doesn't feel right. I smell his stale, sour breath. Up close his eyes are red and damaged-looking; he needs a shave and a shower.

"I've been for a walk on the wild side, Erica," he grins.

"Robbing minimarts? Killing guys?!" Wild side. Just what I was thinking when I had goofy little non-Christian thoughts. Not killing people. That's the wild side plus....

"I'm loving it," Scooter says. "It's so...different from what I've been. It's like I've been...born again!" He laughs uproariously and Adonna throws him an irritated glare. I don't think she likes Scooter very much. So much for the hooking up with an old flame idea. Maybe they can have conjugal visits when they're in the penitentiary.

"Scooter," I say, trying to be firm. "I don't know what's happened to you.

Maybe it was the lightning, but you've got to snap out of it. You're not like these people. You're a...well, you know."

"What?" he asks, grinning madly. "A faggoty suburbia guy? Not any-more."

"You tell her, Scoot," Handsome Jimmy says. I didn't know he was listen-ing. Adonna glares. They go back to plotting or whatever it is they're up to.

"I think he likes you," I say miserably.

Scooter nods. "Yeah. I think so, too. Birds of a feather, all that, you know?" He blinks too fast, too eager, too...weird.

"You're not like them," I repeat quietly.

"What *am* I like?" he asks.

"You're Scooter. You're sweet and gentle, you're a sports nut and an ex-band fag, you're...you."

"Boring," he says. He waves off my little proclamation like it's the dumb-est thing in the world.

I lower my voice so Adonna won't hear. "Why did you kill this Randy guy?"

"Self defense," he says. "It just happened. He didn't like me very much." There's that giggle again.

"And the armed robbery?"

He grins and shrugs. "I...went along with Adonna. It was fun. We stole a car, too. Got it in a campground while the people were off fishing."

"This is insane! Stealing and robbery. Scaring innocent people to death? Did you point guns or anything?"

"At the minimarts? Nah. It's surprising what people will do if you act threatening."

"I can't believe this. You and Adonna conned your way through robbery?"

"Adonna looks pretty scary when she wants to."

I resist the urge to comment on that since she looks like something from hell *all* the time.

"Scooter, you're on the surveillance cameras. They'll figure out who you are. You could go to prison!"

Scooter stands and takes my hand. "C'mon outside."

"Why?"

"I wanna show you something."

I reluctantly follow him out the door. As I look back, Handsome Jimmy smiles at me and Adonna scowls. I feel bad about her face and all, but jeez, she needs to lighten up.

Scooter pulls me out to the old, broken-down corral. He points up at the sky. "Look," he orders.

I look up. It's dark, inky dark, except for the canopy of stars. Funny. They seem brighter than I've ever noticed. But then, maybe it's because I never bother to look up at the sky at home. It's cold out. My breath frosts, and the icy little cold fingers already have worked their way under my shirt, clutching at my boobs like...

Hmmm. Like what? Since I've tossed of religion for the time being, maybe I should think colorfully. Like...a horny preacher. Jimmy Swaggert. *Internal giggle.* I'm as bad as Scooter. Next thing you know I'll be robbing mini-marts.

"So," I say. "Sky. Pretty. Let's go back inside. It's cold."

"You're missing the point, Erica! Look at it. Look hard!"

"I don't know—"

"You know. I know you know. You can feel it."

"Feel what?"

"We're free, Er. Totally, one hundred percent free. No more of the old bullshit that seemed to matter so much before."

"Like kids and jobs and...real life?" I ask. He's scaring me because I'm starting to understand what he's talking about.

He turns and smiles. It's the old Scooter smile, without the twitchy, out-law, lightning-struck strangeness. But what he's saying....

"We can't run away, Scooter. I was wrong to even suggest this idiotic scheme. Like I said before...we're not like them."

"We can do anything we want. Anything."

He takes my hand. I don't know what to do. I've thought about this, sure, but now, I don't know. It doesn't feel right. I'm married to Eric, like it or not, and I've got a slew of E-named rugrats and, and....

I'm kissing Scooter. Kissing hard, our arms thrown around each other and we're making out like we should've back in high school but never did. He presses against me, I press back, I can feel him getting hard and I don't know, this is wrong, we're not free, *we're not!*

"Well now, take a look at this."

I pull away from Scooter, leaving a dangle of commingled spit on my chin. Handsome Jimmy stands at the door, hands in his pockets, grinning like he's just seen the funniest thing in the world.

"What's that husband gonna say about this, Erica?" Handsome Jimmy asks.

"It's nothing," I say in a choked, harsh voice. Scooter looks at me with surprise.

"Nothing?" he asks.

"I don't know," I say.

"When you two finish your business, me and Adonna want to have a little conversation with you."

I try to give Scooter a look that will make him understand. A look that will say "Sorry. Mistake. You know how it is." But whatever look I give him doesn't get the message across, because all he's doing now is grinning goofily and acting like another make-out session is minutes away. Would it be possible for me to screw this up any more? Maybe if somebody got me pregnant, or I go on a minimart shooting spree.

I hurry back inside. Having a fun chat with Handsome Jimmy and Adonna is the lesser of two evils. If I stay outside with Scooter, who knows what will happen? With him in his new, look-at-the-stars mode I could be doing something even stupider than kissing him. Because the kiss was nice. Really nice. And I wanted more.

I'm gonna fry in hell.

I flop onto the couch and wait for Scooter to come back inside. Adonna lights another Marlboro and makes an obviously too-hard effort not to bother looking at me. She studies the smoke curling up to the light bulb above the kitchen table. Handsome Jimmy's still outside with Scooter. Probably comparing notes on how best to pry me away from Eric and my family.

"You really fucked up, girl," Adonna says. She still doesn't look at me.

"Excuse me?"

"You heard me, bitch. Got Scooter tangled up in nasty shit, got yourself tangled up with...what's he say his name is, Jimmy?"

"Isn't that his name?" I ask. Incredulous. He's Handsome Jimmy. Who else could he be?

"If you say so," Adonna says. She finally looks at me with her monster's face. I can't tell if she's grinning or snarling or the scarring has just left a permanent sneer on her. Her voice and 'tude are all I need.

"Yeah," she continues. "Nice job, Erica. I've never understood why people like you don't just mind your own business. Live your fucking boring little lives. But you always gotta stick your suburbia noses into other people's business. And then I guess you religious types are even worse, aren't you? Sure that you're always right, sure that Jesus is on your side. What a bunch of bullshit."

"I made a mistake, okay?"

"What do you plan on doing about it?"

"I don't know."

"Better start thinking. Because things are gonna get a whole lot more complicated before you know it."

I should just jump in the minivan and go home. I should forget about these people—Scooter included—and leave. I can't live everybody else's life for them, I can't fix all the mistakes, I can't make Scooter back into the way he was, and really, when you think about it, is his change really my fault? He's an adult, he made the choice to come after Adonna, he decided to be a bandfag outlaw.

It wasn't my fault. It *isn't* my fault.

"I'm going home," I say, surprising myself and Adonna as I get up and move to the door.

"Good riddance," she snorts.

But as I grab the doorknob the door swings open and smacks me in the forehead. Handsome Jimmy and Scooter are back.

"Sorry," Handsome Jimmy drawls. Grinning. Always grinning at me. "You goin' somewhere?"

"I think she was getting outa Dodge," Adonna says.

"Probably not such a good idea," Handsome Jimmy says. Still grinning. With that slightly sinister undercurrent that lurks underneath his amiable smile so much of the time. Scooter peeks in from behind Handsome Jimmy like a goofy, little-kid sidekick.

"Why would you want to leave, Er?" Scooter asks.

"Because I have a family. And this is...wrong."

"Let her go," Adonna says.

Nobody does anything for a moment. Handsome Jimmy studies me; I imagine I see disappointment in his eyes. Scooter, looking like a puppy begging for a milkbone, gazes at me. He wants to kiss again. I can tell.

I don't know him anymore. Maybe it was the lightning. Or maybe he was always unhinged, but he just kept it hidden until he hooked up with Adonna and killed Randy.

Whatever. I'm going home.

Handsome Jimmy slowly moves to the side of the door. He holds out his arm and gestures for me to go. He gives Scooter a firm little shove back. A clear path to the minivan. I can leave, go home to my husband and children, make things right—or at least try—and go back to the way things were. Without Scooter, of course. He's on his own now. Doing whatever he thinks is right. But at the very least I should offer.

"C'mon, Scooter. Let's go home."

"Don't have a home anymore, Er," he says with that really annoying little giggle he's developed.

"Please," I beg. "Please come home."

Scooter shrugs. "I don't think so."

I tried. I really tried.

I walk past them without a second glance and climb into the minivan.

I bounce over the dusty dirt road back to the highway. I hesitate, because I'm still not a hundred percent sure I want to go back to Eric. Maybe I should try to change Scooter, maybe I should try to help.

Maybe....

I belong with my kids. I realize that now. And God forgive me for what I started with Scooter. But the ball's in his court, and he has to decide what to do. I can't make him leave. I can't make him come back to a life of living in our trailer and cashing unemployment checks. Maybe being a bandfag outlaw is better for him.

But then there's Handsome Jimmy. What do I feel about him? I could...I could....

What? He's a criminal whose name isn't even Jimmy. I don't belong. I have to go home.

To my children. Family.

Eric.

Church.

Pastor Ernie.

Stultifying boredom.

It's where I belong. I have to go back. It's my duty.

I sit at the crossroad. A semi roars past, its wind shaking the minivan. And still I don't move.

I have to go home.

I must.

And I will.

But maybe not just yet....

Eric

Chapter Twelve

Praise Jesus, most holy redeemer. Praise be to the Lord Jesus Christ, may He keep His daughter Erica safe from the distractions and evils of the world. And may He give me strength to do what I must do.

Last night Erica called me. From New Mexico. Oh my Lord sweet God her voice was like an angel's hosanna.

"Hi," she said. She sounded tired to me.

"Erica!" I couldn't think of anything else to say.

"I'm in New Mexico."

The way she said it was like...I don't know. I wasn't sure if she meant she was there to stay. I didn't say anything right away because I didn't know what to say. So I silently said a prayer. Jesus would help us through this. I'd had long talks with Pastor Ernie since Erica left, and he assured me that the Son of God was with me and Satan would leave Erica. I hoped he was right.

Eli tugged at my pants, and the other children made noise in the playroom. "Mommy?!" Eli asked.

I nodded. "Eli misses you," I told her. She didn't say anything, but it sounded like maybe she gasped back the beginning of tears. That was a good sign, I decided.

"I...tell Eli I love him," she said.

"Are you coming home? You can tell him yourself."

Another long silence. Another chance for me to beseech almighty God to heal our temporarily broken family. Pastor Ernie had said pray, pray, PRAY! You can never pray too much.

Sweet Jesus, giver of life and savior, please bring your daughter Erica home—

"I don't think I believe in God anymore, Eric," she said.

PRAYPRAYPRAY!

"At least not the way you do," she added. "I don't know how I feel about anything anymore."

Even though praying felt like the right thing to do, I knew I needed to talk to her. Gently. To somehow bring her back to Jesus.

"I forgive you, Erica," I said. Pastor Ernie said I needed to tell her that she was forgiven. "And I'm sure Jesus forgives you, too."

"Didn't you hear what I said?"

"I—"

"I don't think I believe in God anymore."

"You don't mean it." I was aghast and having a hard time talking to her and praying at the same time. My thoughts got jumbled up. I think I might have told God to repent. Not good. Not good at all. I don't know how truly holy people do it. I've never been able to do or think about more than one thing at a time. It worked great when I was quarterback, because I could focus entirely on completing a pass and not notice that the defensive end was going to cream me. It didn't work so great at the distributorship when I was trying to manage drivers, make my Anhueser-Busch order, and figure out all the tax laws I had to follow. I'm a focused kind of guy. That's why I love Jesus so much. It's easy to focus only on Him.

"You're praying, aren't you?" Erica asked.

"Or course I'm praying! I'm praying for you!" It probably came out sounding snotty and self-righteous, but Erica needed to hear the truth. I don't know what's got into her. I was beginning to think that Scooter, God bless him, had somehow corrupted her. I love Scooter like a brother, and I know Erica does, too, but I think he's been neglecting God for too long and maybe Satan's gained a foothold. I'll have to have a talk with him when he gets back. I've been putting it off for a long time, but it's time for Scooter's redemption. Pastor Ernie told me many times that we needed to constantly add to our flock. It's the way Jesus wants it.

"I'm not sure I want to come back to you. Not the way you are," Erica said.

"What?"

"You're too...holy. I've gone along for years, but I don't think I want to anymore."

I felt myself go pale. I looked down at little Eli. He knew something was up. He stared up at me, unmoving, his big blue eyes filled with fear. I didn't know what to say, so I put the phone down to Eli. "SayhitomommyEli!" I told him, and while he burbled and babbled unintelligible gibberish to his runaway mother, I tried to think, tried to focus, tried to decide what to do. Because I needed to act quickly, or I was going to lose Erica.

I wished I had enough time to call Pastor Ernie and have his counsel, but time was of the essence. I knew that when Eli finally ran out of cooing babble I'd have to say something, do something, to get my wife back.

Eli started to cry, and seemed to be finished talking. I slowly lifted the phone back to my ear. Erica was crying at the other end.

"Come home," I ordered sternly. It was time to take charge, to be the head of the family, just like the bible says.

"No," she whispered.

"Is there...someone else?" I asked. I don't know why I asked, I knew there wasn't, but I didn't know what else to say.

"No. Maybe. I don't know."

"Maybe!? Who?"

A long silence. Just her sniffles and my gaspy anger. Finally, I asked: "Scooter?"

"I don't think so."

"Then who?"

"Nobody. Never mind."

"Tell me where you are, Erica."

"I already told you. New Mexico."

"What are you doing there?"

"It's where Scooter and Adonna are."

"Are you with them?"

"Not anymore."

"Come home."

"No."

"Then I'm coming down."

"Whatever."

"I'm coming to get you. I'm coming to bring you home."

"I don't know."

"Yes. Yes I am. Where exactly are you?"

"Uh...a Motel Six in Silver City. But don't come. Maybe I'll come home. But I still won't believe in God."

She sounded so strange. I wondered if she was drugged. I had to go to her, to help her back into the Lord's light, to bring her home to her family. It was a...rescue.

"I'm coming down. We'll talk. Stay there."

"I don't know. I don't know what I'm going to do. I thought I was coming home, but now I'm not sure."

"Where are Scooter and Adonna now?"

"With Handsome Jimmy, but I'm not sure it's his real name. And I think they're going to probably rob some more minimarts. Scooter got hit by lightning. And Adonna's a disfigured drug addict."

"*Stay right there, I'm coming to get you!*"

"The kids are okay? Eli sounded sad."

"Of course he's sad, he misses him mother. But sure, yeah, they're okay. As well as can be expected."

"That's good."

She had a dreamy quality in her voice. "I'm coming down to get you, Erica."

"I don't believe in God anymore," she said, and then she hung up.

It was stupid to take a delivery truck, but it was the only transportation I could dig up at the last minute. I got my mom to babysit the kids, and now I'm bouncing along a deserted highway in the middle of nowhere to go get my wayward wife.

It's hot and dusty and dry out here, and the truck doesn't have air conditioning, so I'm sweating. But maybe the sweat isn't entirely the heat. I'm sweating the thought of what to say to Erica.

Give me strength, Lord. Give me strength.

I don't know why she doesn't love the Lord as much as I do. I've known for a long time that she has just gone along. I always thought that as time passed she'd see the majesty of Jesus, of faith, and that she'd believe as much as I do. I thought if we had enough kids that the miracle of creating life would convince her, would fill her with faith. But deep down inside I knew it didn't.

Sometimes Erica says things, and she thinks I don't notice that she's subtly making fun of me. I don't think she thinks I'm very smart. You never live down being a jock, no matter how long you live and how hard you try to change the perceptions. One of the things I love most about Erica, have always loved, is her wise-guy-ness. It's the first thing that caught my eye back in high school. She wasn't impressed with me like all the other girls. Back then, I could have anybody. And since I hadn't found the Lord yet, I took advantage of it. I lived a dissolute and corrupt life. But one day Erica caught my eye, and I've never been able to stop looking at her since.

Sometimes I think I love her too much. We both knew that there was trouble in our marriage. When Jane dumped Scooter it made me think. Nothing's forever. Except God, of course. But I think Erica started thinking about us, about our lives and how she wasn't...happy.

I hate to admit it, but I know it's true. It's been true for a long time. Erica isn't happy with her life. I hoped we could straighten things out with Pastor Ernie's help, I really wanted to work on things. But she took off after Scooter.

And now here I am, driving along in a miserably uncomfortable beer delivery truck and she's in New Mexico and I don't know what I'm going to do when I get to her. I'll demand that she obey me. I'm the pillar of the family. I'm the head. I'll tell her, "You are my wife, you will come home to me and our children and that's that." And she'll laugh at me. There's no way I can pull it off. I don't have the power, the gravity, to force her to do anything. It's the problem that underlies everything: Erica's too smart.

Maybe, if Scooter's still down there, I can get him to help. Whatever Erica's babbling about robbing minimarts and lightning—and I still have no idea what she was talking about—Scooter's a good guy. He'll help me out. He knows that Erica and I belong together forever in the eyes of Christ, and he'll help me convince her. It's strange, but Erica respects him more than me. I don't know why. It must be because they go back so far.

Jesus, my light and salvation, bring Erica back to me. I need her. I know that now.

I drive on.

I'll get her back.

The red rock country is beautiful. We should retire down here, play some golf. Have the kids bring their kids and live our golden years in bliss. I could start a church, become Pastor Eric. I like the ring to that. "Pastor Eric." I could do it. People would listen to me.

Maybe. Maybe not. Pastor Ernie has the gift, he can move you, make you think, make you love the Lord. I wonder if I could do it. I'm pretty sure. I don't know, though. If Erica leaves me that makes it harder to deliver the message. We're all sinners, sure. But to lead it helps to have a clean background. Just goes down better to the followers. And if I can't move Erica, if I can't bring her to love Jesus as much as I do, could I minister to others? Maybe it's a stupid idea. Maybe I'm just a follower. There's nothing wrong with being a follower. Not everybody can lead. It's just that it would be nice to be respected, to be admired, to be able to help others. I suppose I'm admired now, but that's only because I'm a businessman, the guy who provides the beer. Great legacy. Mr. Beer. High school jock turns beer-seller. Marries a woman smarter than him, has a bunch of kids, wife runs off to do God-only-knows-what. Yeah. Great.

Loser.

I'm a loser.

It must be because God's testing me. Satan is involved somehow, that's for sure. I'm in the middle of a titanic struggle between good and evil. It's the ultimate test of my life, my being. My faith.

Well, I've got a message for you, Prince of Darkness. You're not gonna beat me. I *will* triumph over you.

Silver City's a nice little town, high desert pretty, with a small college and lots of artsy places downtown. I wonder if I could buy out the beer distributorship?

I drive to the motel where Erica said she was staying. I park, and the motel manager peers curiously at the truck. Probably wondering if she's going to be getting an unexpected beer delivery.

I get out of the truck, stiff and sore, stretch, and slowly, very slowly, walk to the office. I'm here to get Erica, and suddenly I'm scared. What if she refuses to come home?

"Hi," I say to the manager, an older Hispanic woman. She still eyes me curiously. "I'm not delivering anything," I add, and she seems relieved.

"Can I help you?" she asks.

"Could you please ring Erica Stabler's room for me?"

"I believe she checked out," the manager says, tapping her computer keyboard.

"Wonderful. Do you know where she went?"

The woman eyes me. She has a fat face and a skinny body. Weird combination. I suppose since I'm driving an out-of-state beer truck and I haven't shaved or showered in two days I'm looking a little shifty.

"I don't know. And if I did I couldn't tell you."

"Thanks."

I go outside and look up into the clear, cobalt blue sky. Sure is pretty down here. There's a different smell in the air, a desert smell of dryness and junipers and....

Betrayal.

Is that what betrayal smells like? Fresh and dry and clean? No. I must be mistaken.

Now what? *Lord Jesus, show me the way. Give me your holy guidance as to what I should do next.*

And as I finish the prayer, I see our minivan turning down a street a block away. I'm sure it's ours, even at this distance. I recognize the wheel covers, I ordered custom rims since owning a minivan was such an embarrassment that I had to do something to add to the cool factor. Not that custom rims can make a minivan cool, but hey, I may be religious but I'm a guy and that's what guys do.

I leap into the truck, jam it into gear, and roar off after Erica. Luckily, it's such a sleepy little town that I have no problem catching up to her. But instead of getting right behind, honking, flashing lights, getting her to pull over, I hang back. Following.

I want to see where she's going. I feel like a spy. It's probably a sin.

But I stay back.

I'm spying on my wife.

I start to pray, because I'm afraid of what I'll find out.

Chapter Thirteen

This is stupid.

I'm sitting alongside a rural road, a mile behind Erica. I have to stay this far back or else she'll know something's up.

She drove aimlessly for an hour, circling back roads through scrubby hills and canyons. I don't think she was looking for anything, and I'm pretty sure she didn't know I was back here.

I think she was just driving around. Maybe thinking. Or praying. I hope she was praying to almighty God for help.

Now I watch. The minivan is parked far in the distance. I don't think she's gotten out. She's just waiting for something.

Should I make a move? I pray for counsel but none comes. I'm not sure what to do. I start praying, but I'm not sure what to pray for anymore. I'm so tired. I've driven and driven and driven but I haven't slept. As I pray I nod off, weird thoughts intrude, my prayers jump to strange visions of baby pigs and Budweiser bottles, pray, nod off, pray, pray....

Erica's gone when I wake up. It's late afternoon. I've been sleeping for hours.

Shit. I don't like to use or think foul language anymore, but if ever there was a "shit" moment, this is it.

I don't know what to do.

I pray.

Shit.

Maybe I'll go back to that motel and get a room. Maybe Erica will go back there. I'll call home and see if Mom has heard from her.

I fire up the rumbling beer truck and drive.

The only problem: now I'm lost. Double shit.

I turn down a bumpy dirt road toward a little, ramshackle ranch house nestled under a red butte wall. I can't tell if anybody's home, but I'll give it a shot. Maybe I can get some directions how to get out of here.

I've really screwed this up. Be strong, Eric! Trust the Lord! Pray to almighty God to guide you to your wife and your life!

I park in front of the ranch house. No sign of life. If there's anybody here, they're probably wondering why the beer man is coming to visit. I should've brought a full truck so I could offer gifts to the natives.

I get out and head to the front door, less than convinced that I'll find anybody home. I knock on the door. It rattles and shakes like it's going to fall down, but there's no response. I knock again, then turn to go back to the truck. A squeak. The door opens.

"Hi Eric," Scooter says.

I spin around toward him. He's leaning against the doorjamb. He looks weird, disheveled and dirty, with a wild-eyed stare and spooky-looking expression.

It takes me a minute to realize what's happened to him: Satan has taken hold!

"Scooter!" I say, trying to sound normal but every alarm in my mind screaming warning. "Are you okay?"

"Never better, Eric," he says. He giggles strangely.

"Erica said something about lightning. And hold-ups."

Scooter laughs. "My life's gotten interesting. C'mon in."

He goes back inside. I hesitate. If he's filled with Satan I could be in danger, but then again, I'm a righteous man, so my natural godliness should fight off any Satanic proddings. Besides, I have to minister to Scooter and bring him back.

I follow him inside. The place is dark and dingy. Scooter flops down on a sprung couch and lounges. Grinning.

"Got any brewskis in that truck?"

"Nope. Running empty."

"Why you down here?"

"I came to get Erica."

"Oh."

The smug smile he's been beaming at me fades. "Do you know where she is, Scooter?"

"Eric," he says, leaning forward. "Have you ever had a life-changing epiphany?"

"Sure. When I found the Lord and savior Jesus Christ."

Scooter sighs. "Yeah. Of course. I forgot about that. But what about non-religious? What about a complete change of outlook on the world? Ever have one of those?"

"Only when Jesus—"

"Gotcha." Scooter studies me. It's the strangest thing. He's like somebody who resembles the Scooter I used to know, but a different person. It reminds me of those times when you'll be walking down the street and think you see somebody familiar, but when you get closer it turns out to be just a resemblance. And sometimes not all that close of a resemblance. That's how it is with Scooter now. The guy sitting on the saggy couch is a sixty-percent match for Scooter Biffman.

"What's happened to you?" I ask.

"Told you. A life-changing epiphany."

"What?"

"I'm not Scooter Biffman anymore."

"I can see that," I say cautiously. "Who are you now?"

Scooter stares off into the mid-distance in the dim light. I glance around, checking for signs of Erica. I want to help Scooter, but I want to find Erica, too. I'll do this for a few minutes, then get down to the important business.

"Who are you, Scooter?" I repeat softly.

He looks back at me with a chilling coldness that shakes me to my soul. "You probably think I'm the devil, don't you?" he asks.

"No."

"Sure you do. I know how all that bible humping stuff you believe in makes you think."

I start to object at his coarse vulgarity, but then think better of it. Best to let Satan speak through Scooter before I try to oust the beast.

"No little devils here, Eric. Just a new outlook. I'm moving on from sports-dweeb, bandfag, suburbia lawn-mowing Scooter Biffman. Now...let's say I'm a road warrior. Like Mel Gibson in the old movie. Or a nomad. Maybe that's a better description."

"And how will you support yourself?" I ask. It's the first question that comes to my mind.

"Who gives a fuck?" Scooter sneers. I feel like a dope. Satan has a stronger grip than I realized.

"Scoot—"

"I mean, really Eric. Lose the fuckin' middle-class horseshit 'What about my 401-k?' attitude. I don't want to be one of those pathetic losers who busts his ass all his life, retires, and has a heart attack on the second day of the retirement he's waited for all his life. That's not a life, Eric. It's a...prison sentence."

"It's the way of the world, Scooter."

"Not my world. Not anymore."

I'm not sure how to proceed. Satan is such a clever adversary. I wish Pastor Ernie was here. He'd know what to do.

"You can't just wander, Scooter. Your life needs structure."

"Why?"

"Because."

"You need to do better than that, Eric."

Okay. I probably should pray, but right now I need to keep talking. Keep Scooter talking.

"What about Crystal?"

Scooter's expression changes. Softens. Of course, how could I have been so stupid?! His daughter would be the one thing to reach past Satan's claws and into his heart.

"Crystal's...not relevant," he says, his voice catching.

"She's your daughter, Scoot. She always will be."

"She hates me. And it doesn't matter anymore. Dr. Dwyane the periodontist is who she's calling daddy now. The kid can't stand me. So be it. That's the way it goes. Can't do anything about it."

He says it, but I don't believe it. I can tell he's faking. His voice isn't sure.

"You shouldn't quit on her, Scooter. It's just a phase. She's confused, she's—"

"—History," he says. *Satan* says.

I know I should continue working on him, I know I should minister and try to release him from the demon's grasp and bring him back to the light of Christ. But I'm suddenly weary and unsure and I want Erica back. I'll work on Scooter another time.

"Where is she?" I ask.

He's momentarily confused. "Crystal?"

"Erica."

Scooter grins. "Oh. Yeah. Guess that's why you're here, huh?"

"Where is she?" I say, surprised at how threatening my voice sounds. Hard and cruel, just like I used to sound when some defensive end would sack me and taunt and I'd say, "You may have sacked me this time, asshole, but I'm gonna whup your ass, you loser." It had a Clint Eastwood quality to it, but I could usually come through on the threat. And that's the way I sound right now. Scooter notices.

"Gonna beat me up if I don't tell you, Eric? Gonna throw a fifty-yard bomb and make me look bad? What will you do?"

I'm as surprised as Scooter is when I lunge at him, grab his throat, and throw him choking to the ground. And I'm ashamed at how good it feels to be squeezing the breath out of him. He fights back at first, but I'm way too strong for him and he soon gives up. His face flushes red, his eyes bulge, and as the movement goes out of him and his skin takes on a bluish tinge, he smiles.

Satan smiles.

And I let go because I realize that this is exactly what the Prince of Darkness wants. He wants me to lose control, to forget about the majesty of God and give in to my violent, base impulses.

When I let go of Scooter he gasps and chokes. It takes a few minutes for him to recover, and as he slowly sits up, rubbing at my fingermarks on his throat, I flop onto the couch and begin to cry. The tears flow freely, I'm not embarrassed, I'm not really sad or scared, I'm just...numb. The tears are tears of frustration and impotence. I want Erica back, I want to save Scooter from the devil, I want my life back.

And I'm crying because I'm not sure that I can ever get it back.

It takes a while for Scooter to be able to speak and for me to stop crying. But eventually we both recover. Scooter isn't angry, isn't vengeful, isn't...anything.

"So," he rasps. "Was that satisfying for you?"

"No."

"Didn't think so. It ain't religious to kill people. Especially old friends."

"Where is she?" I ask.

"I dunno."

"You're lying."

"She kissed me, you know."

I turn to him. I'm completely dumbfounded. Maybe I should've gone ahead and strangled him.

"Yeah, I was a surprised as you. I mean, we go way back and all. And now that I think of it, there was always a little sexual tension there."

"Kissed?"

"Yep. Tongue, too. It was nice."

I start shaking. Ohmygodohmygod, this is worse than I could've imagined.

"But," Scooter says, sighing wistfully, "I don't think it was meant to be. I was into it, don't get me wrong. And so was Erica. But we both came to our senses. Actually, she came to her senses before I came to mine. It was a good wake-up call for her though, I think. What's that horseshit stuff they talk about in business—thinking outside the box? That's what Erica's doing. She's thinking outside the box."

"She committed adultery."

"Only if you consider a little spit-swapping adultery."

"If the heart—"

"Whatever, Eric. I think you have a bigger problem with Erica than a little make-out session with me. There's this guy Jimmy. That's not his real name, but it's what he calls himself this week."

I'm so stunned by all of this it's hard to speak. My voice chokes in my squeezed throat, I'm trying to absorb, pray, think, and I'm not doing anything. I'm not sure I'm still alive. No, I'm still alive...I'm burning with jealousy. That's another of Satan's best friends. If he can infect you with jealousy, he can make you do anything. *Oh God, protect me from....*

Fuck this prayer shit. "Who the fuck's Jimmy?!"

"Hmmm. You're turning into a toilet mouth all of a sudden. Good, very good. See, thinking outside of the box."

"WHO IS HE?!"

Scooter rubs his neck and sighs. For the first time since I've been here, he reminds me of the old Scooter.

"He's everything you're not, Eric," he says softly. He tells me a long, convoluted story about this Jimmy character. He sounds like a white-trash outlaw jailbird who should be locked up for good.

"And the funny thing is," Scooter says as he finishes up the story, "is that I think Erica might be a little in love with the guy."

Scooter couldn't have hurt me more if he'd knifed me in the heart.

"You'd like him," Scooter adds, and I feel my hands twitching with the desire to wring his neck. "He's kind of majestic. Been around, done a lot of different things. But he's real cool. Reminds me of you in high school."

"She loves him?" I croak.

"Well, maybe love is too strong a word. It's hard to tell what anybody's really thinking, you know. But I think she might be infatuated with him. Walk on the wild side and all."

Walk on the wild side?! Satan has a firm grip on my wife's soul. We may need to do an exorcism when I get her back. We'll definitely have a prayer circle going full-time.

"The thing you've never understood about Erica," Scooter says, that smugness creeping back, "is that she's a natural born hellraiser. Until you whupped her—"

"I never touched her!"

"Metaphorically speaking. Until you crammed Jesus down her throat and turned her into a breeder, she was gonna be something special."

"She is something special. She's a wife and mother."

"Yeah, well, I mean maybe something other than that."

"What?"

"Who knows? She never had the chance."

"That's liberal humanist claptrap."

Scooter sighs like I'm the stupidest dolt in the world. Maybe I am.

"Spare me the Pat Robertson baloney. Erica's stifled, she has been forever. And this Jimmy guy revved her up a little. Made her feel like a woman."

"She's had...." I have to think for a second. "Seven kids! How much more womanly could she feel?"

Scooter sighs again. I sound stupid even to myself, so it's understandable that he's not going to bother to argue anymore. We sit in silence. Scooter seems quite content to sit here and stare at the wall. I think he's on drugs.

"Are you alone?" I finally ask.

"For the time being. They're out, uh, picking up groceries."

"Adonna?"

"Yeah. She's not quite what you remember."

"And this Jimmy character?"

"Jimbo too. You gonna hang around and meet 'em?"

"Is Erica with them?"

"I'm not sure."

"You're lying."

Scooter grins. "Yeah. I am."

"Tell me."

"Erica went with them."

"To get groceries?"

"You could say that."

"Scooter...." I stand up and move toward him. He looks a little frightened. Good. It's about time I take control.

"What?"

"I'm taking Erica back. She's my wife, she can't do this."

"She can do anything she wants, Eric. She's not your slave. But it's none of my business. It's between you and her."

"How come you're not with them?" I ask.

Scooter smiles cryptically. "Four's a crowd."

"Meaning?"

"You don't want to know."

"Where are they?!" I move toward Scooter and he flinches. It takes every fiber of my discipline not to kill him. He's been like a brother for as long as I can remember, but right now he's the enemy, one of Satan's minions who's destroying my family.

"They're...looking for someplace to rob."

"*They're what?!*"

"Told you you didn't want to know. Adonna and Jimmy and Erica are picking up groceries. And a little cash. Without paying for it."

My head spins, it's like I've got the stomach flu and every meal I've had for the last twenty-four hours is fighting for a way to blast out of my guts onto the floor. I can't speak for a moment, maybe I'm going to throw up on Scooter, but then the wave of nausea passes. My vision's blurred, my throat thick, filled with a vile mix of horror and revulsion.

"They...forced her?"

"Sorry. She came back here—we thought she'd gone home—and she said, well...."

"What'd she say?"

"She said, 'I want to know what it's like.' Surprised the hell outa all of us, because when she took off before she was lecturing everybody on the importance of clean, honest living. Kinda like you. But then she came back and what do you know, Erica wants to taste the life of the petty criminal. Pretty weird, huh? I'll never understand people. I know Erica better than anybody I've ever known, and she surprised the shit outa me with that one."

My God.... She's completely lost her mind. She's sinning beyond anything I could've imagined. Adultery, theft, how many other commandments has she broken? And what will I tell the kids when she's sitting in some women's prison? We'll get her off, we'll hire a good lawyer, prove that these psychopaths brainwashed her, kind of what happened to Patty Hearst, sure, it's like that whole mess. And Scooter, well, maybe he's been brainwashed, too, but as much as I once loved Scooter, now he's the enemy. If I have to take Scooter down to save Erica, that's what I'll do.

"We need to go find her."

"I told you, Eric, I don't know—"

"We're going to get her. And I'm going to bring her home," I say. "She belongs with me."

Scooter doesn't argue. A small smile creeps across his face. "It's a big world. She could be anywhere."

"Were they coming back?" I ask.

"It doesn't work that way with these people," Scooter says. "It's more...free-form. But I assume they'll be back. Hope so. I'm stranded, otherwise. Besides, even though she won't admit it, I think Adonna's fond of me. I killed her ex-husband, you know."

I can't begin to deal with what Scooter's saying. Instead, I grab his arm and drag him outside to the beer truck.

We're going to find Erica.

I'm putting a stop to this nonsense.

I'm taking her home, and we're going to spend the rest of our lives praying for forgiveness.

Chapter Fourteen

We drive.

I'm not sure I can trust Scooter. In fact, I *know* I can't trust him. He sits, chattering about nothing, while we cruise the interstate, pulling off at every ramp with a minimart or gas station, looking for Erica and her...what should I call them? Gang?

"So the thing is," Scooter is saying as we slowly drive through yet another AM/PM Minimart lot, "is that you just never know. You can go all your life doing the supposed right thing, then BAM!, you get hit by lightning, and everything changes." He giggles that annoying giggle and I want to strangle him.

"Shut up."

"No need to get surly. If you haven't reached my state of understanding, I realize it's a tough thing to comprehend."

"Shut up."

"It's like what the Buddhists say about right mind," he continues, ignoring me. "You have to live in the here and now. You can't control tomorrow, or even the next minute. Live in the now."

"That's just...just bullshit!"

"Wow, see you've changed. I've never heard you cuss so much."

"You can't live your life without planning. You can't just let things happen. That's what Satan wants."

"Oh, fuck Satan."

"I agree with you there."

"And fuck God, too."

He's gone too far. I pull the truck over, put it in park, and glare at Scooter. I hope I look as threatening as I feel. "You don't say anything like that to me ever again. If you do, I'll kill you. Do you understand?" I've never threatened to kill anyone before. It feels good. But I'm doing it for a moral, ethical reason. We must protect God from blasphemy.

"Chill out," Scooter says. He's not reacting the way I'd hoped. Maybe since I already tried to kill him once today, my threat doesn't carry as much weight. He's not afraid of dying.

"I mean it."

"And I mean it too, Eric. Stop being a spaz. Okay, you're religious boy. Great. Glad it makes you happy. Just don't jam it down my throat. Or Erica's."

"Erica freely chose the way of Christ."

"Maybe. And now she's having second thoughts."

"You can't have second thoughts about salvation!"

"So we find her," Scooter says as the air conditioner starts blowing warm air. I need to get moving again, but I can't make myself drive just yet. *Fuck*

God. Just the words have frozen me. I'm afraid that Scooter is beyond salvation. "And she and Jimmy and Adonna are sucking up purloined Yoo-Hoo and chewing burgled Ho-Hos. What do you do?"

"Take her home."

"She doesn't want to go. All of a sudden, Erica's just like me. She wants a taste of something different from home-schooling kids and prayers and you. She says, 'Eric, I love you, but I don't want to live with you for awhile. Maybe anymore. I have to find out why I'm here, what life's about, how it feels to take stuff from minimarts and be on the run'. What do you do, Eric?"

"This is a stupid conversation. You're filled with evil."

"What do you do?" he repeats. The power has shifted to Scooter. I'm scared, I feel small. Sweat pops out on my forehead and tickles as it slowly moves toward my eyebrows. I'm so afraid.

"Pray," I whisper. "Pray for help. For the Lord to guide Erica."

Scooter shrugs. "I suppose that's as good as anything. Because I don't think she's gonna come with you. Even if you try to force her. To say nothing of Jimmy."

My throat slams shut. *Evil, evil, evil.* And this Jimmy person is the focal point of it all. He's lured Erica away from me. "What's he gonna do?" I ask when I can speak again.

"Hard to say. He's a cool guy, but I get a little feeling of crazy under the surface with him. Maybe even violence, you know? Same thing with Adonna, but you can see it on her face." He laughs, and I'm not sure why. Scooter giggles and laughs inappropriately a lot since I've found him. It's like he's privy to some private joke and he won't let anybody else in on it.

"Erica is my wife. This guy has nothing to do with her. With us."

"I think he does now, bro'. Whether you like it or not, your life is in serious upheaval. Feels good, don't it?" Scooter grins at me. The grin is the

Scooter of old, but behind it lies...Satan. I know I sound like a broken record, but I can't help it. My life, my world, has become saturated with Satan. The evil one is in every nook and cranny and friendly grin.

We drive on. We go twenty miles in either direction on the interstate, stopping at every potential robbery spot, but no sign of Erica and her...crew. Scooter finally shuts up, instead busying himself fiddling with the radio trying to pick up sports scores. He may have become a road warrior outlaw, but the sports reporter geek still lies within.

"Let's get something to eat," he says after giving up on the radio search. "No reason to starve. They're probably back at the house anyway."

I didn't realize I was hungry until he mentioned food, but suddenly I'm famished. I pull off the interstate and roll up to a grubby-looking bar and grill. Looks like a biker joint. But, as the driver of a beer truck, I know that I'm welcome anywhere.

Inside it's the same as all these places are, dark and dank, smoky even though there's only a few patrons, a couple of bedraggled pool tables and a large screen TV tuned to CNN. Ever since the World Trade Center, I've noticed that bars spend less time tuned to sports stuff and more time on the news. The world changes. Satan. Always Satan. The few locals slurping up Buds while they smoke glance our way. The bartender, a handlebar mustachioed shaved-headed hard case with a gold tooth and sneery leer, throws one of those bartender glares that I've seen a million times. For a guy who doesn't drink, I sure know how it feels in these kinds of places. I've made a thousand deliveries to guys like him.

"I didn't place no order," he growls as Scooter and I walk up.

"Just passing through," I say. Scooter and I order a couple of burgers and fries, then wait while Baldy Golden-Tooth throws our orders together. I keep an eye on him to make sure he doesn't spit in them or drop the burgers on the floor. He seems like that kind of person. Filled with Satan. Sometimes you just know.

Scooter watches CNN while he sips a beer. The anchorbabe, tucked into the corner of an annoyingly cluttered screen of stock tickers, mini-headlines, and weather reports, is talking about a fire somewhere in North Carolina. It's only when she mentions something about a ghost town and dead body that I start to listen closely, and then only because Scooter starts choking on his beer and whispering, "Ohfuckshit," over and over.

"Authorities are looking for a missing Forest Service employee, Adonna Moore, ex-wife of the dead man...." the anchorbabe says as the picture shows cops digging in rocky ground. Old buildings and soaring mountain peaks are in the background.

"Is that—"

"Shut up!" Scooter hisses.

The anchorbabe says that Adonna went missing and James Biffman's car was found abandoned on the road to the ghost town. They interview a dorky-looking Forest Service guy, and he gives an incoherent statement about Scooter coming to the visitor center looking for Adonna. The story finishes off on the cheery note that authorities are searching for Scooter and Adonna.

"That's not good," I say, and for some reason it makes me feel better. All of Scooter's outlaw, king-of-the-road baloney is suddenly reduced to a simple fact: the cops want him.

"You killed that guy?" I ask.

"Keep your voice down!" he growls. A couple of locals looked up when I said "killed". But I don't care, because now I have the advantage and it feels good. Scooter's smug grin is long gone.

"Did you?" I say, quieter.

"It was self-defense. The dude was gonna kill me!"

"So why didn't you call the cops right then and there?"

"Because Adonna didn't want to. She was cooking up a batch of meth with the asshole, and besides, she doesn't like the police." Scooter drains his beer and stares miserably at the TV. Amazing how quickly his mood changed. Maybe it's dawning on him he could spend some time in prison with large, muscular people who won't treat him well.

"You should turn yourself in, Scooter. The longer you wait, the worse it'll be."

He jumps up. "Let's go. We've got to find them and warn 'em."

"What about our food?"

"Fuck it. C'mon."

I toss a ten at the surly bartender and we're on our way.

At least Scooter and I are on the same page now. He wants to find them as much as I do, and it's not a big joke to him. As we drive, he sits grimly, no more of his bogus philosophy of the road, the romance of crime, none of that.

Scooter's scared. Good. It's about time.

Scooter sees the minivan before I do.

"There! Parked in front of the Mexican place!"

I jerk the beer truck off the interstate, barely missing a light post and cutting off a Taurus. The Taurus' driver flips me off, and I feel bad that I scared him, but it had to be done.

"Do you suppose they're robbing it right now?" I ask.

"Who knows? They could just be having a number three with beans and rice. Who gives a fuck? We've just got to talk to them. Adonna thought they'd never find Randy's body. This makes it all the more interesting."

I don't like the change in Scooter's attitude. The brief moments of fear at the bar have been replaced by that annoying new outlook of his, the danger-boy let's-see-what-we-can-get-away-with criminal mindset. And now that a murder has been uncovered, I'm horrified at what might happen to Erica. If these clowns pull her down with them....

Scooter's giggling again. "I wonder if Jane's heard yet?" he says. "Bet Dr. Dwayne is scared. Probably thinks I'm gonna come get him." Scooter laughs so hard I think he's gonna cry. "I could show up at the front door and scream "Boo!" and I bet he'd piss in his pants!"

I wish Scooter was the old Scooter, the Scooter I remember. Weak and goosey. Much preferable to this snide, Satan-filled loudmouth. If only Satan could be defeated. Why don't people realize what trouble the Prince of Darkness will lead them to—in Scooter's case, probably prison—why don't they come around to righteousness? It's too bad it takes a slap upside the head for most humans. I feel blessed that the Lord has allowed me to understand without going through something terrible like what's happened to Scooter.

And what's happening to Erica.

Oh God. Erica. I'm not sure what to do.

I park next to our minivan. I take a deep breath, say a quick prayer, and follow Scooter to the door.

Inside it's dark. It smells of chiles and tortillas. Annoying *"Hihihi, arriba!"* music blares, and I have to wait a few seconds for my eyes to adjust to the dim light before I can see anything. A heavy stillness suffuses the restaurant; it's like the air is so filled with Mexican food odors that nothing can move. I scan the booths, looking for Erica. My heart throbs in my ears. I don't know if I've ever been so scared.

"Do you see 'em?" Scooter asks. He's scanning the place, his eyes jerking from table to table. A fair number of lunchtime diners crowd the place, and as I squint looking for Erica, I'm almost relieved when I don't see her. I want her back, but I'm afraid, too.

"Not yet...." But as soon as the words leave my mouth, there she is. In a corner booth with Adonna Moore and the Jimmy guy. It's too dim for me to see them well, and the only reason I spot Erica is because I know her so well. Just the tilt of her head is enough for me to identify her. She's deep in conversation with her new pals. They haven't seen Scooter and me yet.

"There," I whisper to Scooter.

A hostess starts to hand us menus, but Scooter waves her off and heads toward the corner booth. I follow. My positive "I'm gonna get my wife back" resolve melts away. I'm uncertain again, especially as we get closer and I see that this Jimmy guy is strong and good-looking.

Oh shit. I try to pray but I can't. I'm too clogged with fear and jealousy and—

Adonna looks up as Scooter and I walk toward them. Her face is horribly mangled, a nightmare, and I feel my butt clench and stomach quease. Oh God. She's a monster. Erica looks up, but she doesn't smile or frown or anything. She's utterly blank, like I'm a stranger and she's not the least bit interested in who I am or what I want. The Jimmy guy looks blandly at me, a hint of a smile. He doesn't look threatening, but I remember Scooter's words of "violence just below the surface" so I approach with caution.

"What the fuck?!" Adonna snaps. God, she's hideous. I know that we shouldn't judge God's creatures by their looks, and that something terrible happened to her, but she's right out of a monster movie. I don't understand how these guys can eat around her. I've just seen her and I've lost my appetite for the rest of the week.

"Hello, Eric," Erica says. Her voice is flat. Strange. Has Satan taken hold? I can't tell yet, but it doesn't look good.

The Jimmy guy grins broadly. For the white trash hustler that I assume he is, he has perfect teeth. Like movie stars' teeth, even and white and almost too good to be true. I know this kind of guy—glad-handing backslapper, quick to take advantage of his charm to lie, cheat and steal. The perfect vessel for Satan to ply his tricks.

"Well, well, well. The long lost husband," Jimmy says, grinning. I hate him. I hate him with all my being. "I'm Jimmy. Nice to meet you, Eric. Heard a lot about you."

I ignore him and keep my eyes locked on Erica. "C'mon. We're going home."

She won't make eye contact. She looks at Scooter instead of me. "Why did you bring him here?" she asks. It's a knife in the gut. She sounds like I'm some kind of pest.

"We need to make some decisions," Scooter says. "It's all over the news, they found Randy's body, the cops know who we are and they're looking for us." Scooter giggles stupidly. He should be shrill and terrified, but he seems to find it all amusing.

Adonna just smiles. I guess it's a smile. With that monster face it's hard to tell.

"Welcome to our world, Scooter. Fun, ain't it?"

The Jimmy guy grins like Adonna just told the funniest joke in the world. "How's it feel to be a wanted man, Scoot?" At that, Adonna and Jimmy laugh and chuckle and smile knowingly at each other. It's as if they're proud of their boy's first home run in Little League. Even Erica smiles. I can't believe any of this. I've stumbled into one of those crazy dreams, the ones where everything is different and everything's the same and you can't tell whether you're awake or asleep until something really strange happens, like you start to fly or somebody famous shows up and begins to dance. You know the kind I mean.

"What should we do?" Scooter asks. Then he joins in the laughter and frivolity. I can't understand why these freaks are laughing about murder and arrest.

"Dunno," Adonna says. "Wait. Yeah, I do know what I'm gonna do."

"What?" Scooter asks.

"I'm going to Disneyland!" Adonna laughs and I'm sure she's insane. Whatever happened to her face made her crazy. I try to remember her as a 17-year-old from high school, but that was so long ago and so much has changed I can't begin to conjure up a memory of her. Vague, hazy...recollections of those years are too hard. I can only understand the insanity of now. I look at Erica. She's watching me.

"Come home," I say quietly.

"I'm not sure," she replies, just as quiet.

"Really, what are we gonna do?" Scooter says. "They're after you, Adonna. And you're a lot easier to spot than me."

"True," she says. "But I have more experience running. You up to it, Scooter? You ready to live *our* life for the rest of yours?"

"The thing is, Scoot, you can't just dip a toe in and then go back to bein' whatever you were before," Jimmy says. I'll give him credit for one thing: he's making good sense right now. "Once you're in, you're in. You've got two choices, friend. Stay out with us, or go in and hope for the best from the boys in blue. Think they'll give you a fair shake? Think they'll believe you? Think you can go back to the old life with your friends here and your ex-wife and your little girl? That's your choice, Scoot. You got one of them life changing moments right now, right here in this greasy Mexican joint. And you gotta make a quick choice. What's it gonna be?"

"Well—" Scooter hesitates, and I'm hoping he's finally coming to his senses.

"No fair wiggling, Scoot. Gotta make the choice. Quick." Jimmy stares intently at Scooter. I know what he's doing, he's trying to force Scooter to evil. He's trying to corrupt Scooter's immortal soul, to pull him straight into hell. I should intervene, I should stop this, and I know I'll have to answer for it at judgement day that I didn't step up to help. But right now, at this instant, I'm frozen. I can't help, and I'm not sure I want to help. I'm too afraid, and I'm too concerned about Erica. Because I know that she'll be next. They'll want her to decide, and I don't want that to happen, I don't want her to make a choice, because I'm afraid of the choice she'll make.

Scooter is trapped. His eyes dart wildly, and for a moment I think he's going to run. He even starts to move, I expect him to sprint out the door and into the desert, and I wait, and—

He doesn't move. Nothing. Adonna and Jimmy watch. Erica watches. Scooter glances at me, then Erica. Is he frightened? Unsure.

Then—

And then Scooter giggles. The smile returns.

And I know he's lost forever.

And so do Adonna and Jimmy. Jimmy reaches out his hand to Scooter. "Let's shake on it, Scoot. Man to man, *mano a mano*, you're with us now."

Scooter hesitates for the briefest moment, then shakes Jimmy's hand. It feels like a graduation, when the old faculty guy grabs your hand, gives you a diploma, and sends you out into the world. Except Scooter's diploma is a death warrant—or at least a one-way ticket to prison.

Scooter plops down at the booth. And now they're all looking at me, like I don't belong, like I don't understand their impossibly psycho, sinful club. Which I don't. I wait for Erica. I'm not leaving without her. Her expression is impossible to read. I think she's considering. I know that she's not as far-gone as Scooter, I know that her motherly instincts are such that she couldn't possibly desert her children, her gifts from almighty God.

At least I hope so.

Jimmy looks over at her. "How 'bout you, Erica? Right now seems to be the time for choices, maybe you oughta make one, too. Since hubby's here and all."

Erica blushes. Good. At least she's still capable of embarrassment.

"We're going home, Erica. To the children," I say. I'm not sure how to play this, whether to be the Moses-like patriarch demanding compliance, or Mr. Sensitivity and understanding and quietly wheedle her back. Right now I'll stick with motherhood guilt and see if it flies.

Erica hesitates. She looks between me and Jimmy, and the expression, oh my God, she looks at the disgusting hustler with a look that should be reserved *for me!* No warmth, no friendly remembrances. He's a criminal, a liar, and she shouldn't be looking at him this way. He's trying to keep her from her children, from her God-ordained life.

The Mexican restaurant bustles around me, but I'm only aware of a static background of clanking plates, Mariachi music, voices, cash register, phone, blended into a nauseating symphony of discordant sound, this is a nightmare, and Erica's not speaking, not deciding, she's waffling—

And it's now that I realize what I have to do. I have to rescue her from this. I have to protect her, to bring her back to her children and to God. I owe nothing to Adonna and the Jimmy person, they made their choices long ago, and Scooter, well, I will forever feel guilty for what I'm about to do, but it's the right thing, the moral thing, and I've got to do it. What would Jesus do? He'd do what I'm doing.

I pull my cell phone out of my pocket.

And I dial 911.

"Nine-one-one operator. State your location and the nature of your emergency."

"I'm at the El Tecolote restaurant right off the interstate. There are wanted felons here, Adonna Moore and James Biffman. This is an emergency—"

As I'm speaking, Jimmy sighs tiredly, reaches into his coat pocket, and pulls out a gun.

"And they're armed and dangerous," I add. The 911 operator starts asking stuff, but there's no more to say, so I disconnect.

"You really shouldn't have done that, pard'," Jimmy drawls with a smile. He lays the gun on the table. Adonna's eyes dart wildly between the gun and me and Jimmy and.... I stop looking at her because that face is so gross. Why in the world didn't she get it fixed? I try hard to remember what she looked like before, but no matter how much I concentrate I can't get the picture. Doesn't matter, I suppose. But it seems strange that memory is so fragile. It's not like I've got amnesia or something. She must not have made much of an impression in high school.

"What the fuck, Eric?!" Scooter's whining pulls me back into the here and now and away from my Adonna reverie. Strange. It surprises me that I could wander off down an unimportant mental corridor right in the middle of this mess. I look back at Erica. She's the important one here, she's who counts.

I know her well enough to be able read her expression. She's disappointed in me. Why? I'm doing the right thing. These people need to be brought to justice.

"C'mon, Erica," I say. I don't know how many times I'm going to have to say it. Once more, I decide. Then I grab her and drag her out. Since there's a gun on the table, I can only assume that Jimmy plans to make this ugly. I wonder what I'll do if he threatens to kill me? Dying while doing the right thing is martyrdom; I could be in paradise in a matter of minutes.

The thought doesn't console me, however. It shows a true lack of faith that I'm so tied to this world. If I survive this I'm going to have to work on my faith and priorities.

"Gonna stand by your man, Erica?" Jimmy asks. Smiling. The guy's always smiling.

Erica doesn't respond. She's acting so tortured and hesitant that I wonder if she's on drugs.

"Not much time, Erica," Jimmy continues. "Thanks to hubby here we'll be having to do some fancydancing. You game?"

"I don't know," Erica says with an irritating hem and haw in her voice, and I decide that's it. I've had enough.

I reach over the table, grab her arm, and yank her to her feet. She doesn't fight, but she doesn't really come along, either.

I can't say I'm shocked when I find myself looking down the barrel of Jimmy's gun. I've never had a gun pointed at me before, so it's a strange sensation. One finger-twitch away from going home to Jesus. So many regrets; I'll miss the kids. But you can't cling to this life, the bible specifically states that you have to be willing to let go.

"Can't say I like getting between a man and his wife," Jimmy says as restaurant patrons scream and start stampeding the door. "But this is a special case. I'm thinking Erica's conflicted, and I'd hate for her to make a decision she might regret someday."

"What happens between me and my wife is none of your business," I say, trying to keep my voice calm and level. "And a gun isn't going change anything."

"I've found that guns do change things," Jimmy chuckles. "Helps clarify vision."

Scooter's eyes are frisbee-sized, Adonna looks pissed and scared. Jimmy smiles at me, calm as can be. I look at Erica. She's shaking her head.

"This is wrong, Jimmy," she says softly.

"Your choice," Jimmy says. "Just gotta convince me that you're choosin' is the real thing, not coercion." I'm surprised he knows a word as big as "coercion". For an evil one, I think this guy is probably pretty bright.

I let go of Erica's arm. I won't force her, I decide. She needs to do the right thing for the right reasons. She's smart enough and wise enough, she has to be. I can't force her, even though that's what I want to do. It won't work, I realize that now as I look at the business end of Jimmy's gun. You can't force people to do anything. Well, you can force them, but you can't make it stick.

It's suddenly quiet. The restaurant has emptied out, and the only sound is the irritating music and a gurgling fryer back in the kitchen.

"Well?" Jimmy asks Erica.

Silence.

Do the right thing! I scream in my mind. I should pray but I can't.

"I think," Erica says, and we all hang on her words. "I think," she repeats, looking over at me, "that it's time for me to go back to my family."

And the instant she says the words, Jimmy lowers his gun. He smiles.

"Probably for the best, Erica," he says. "Don't think you were cut out for this kind of life." Sirens scream in the distance, coming closer. "You two oughta get along. Hard to say what's gonna happen now. And thanks for making that call, friend," Jimmy says to me, his smile fading.

"C'mon, Scooter," I say. He deserves one last chance to get away from these people.

"Uh-uh," he smiles. "I think I'll play this one out," he says. "It's the fourth quarter, score's tied, fourth and one at the goal with two seconds on the clock. You don't leave the game right now. You stay and see how it ends."

I want to scream some sense into him, but the sirens are almost here, and Erica tugs at my sleeve.

"Let's go, Eric. He's where he wants to be."

We turn to leave. I glance back. The three of them sit in the booth, looking strangely calm. Jimmy sighs, looks down at his gun, then over at Adonna.

"Well?" he asks her. She shrugs. And the last thing I see as Erica and I hurry out the front door is Scooter smiling at his new friends.

Like he's crazy.

Chapter Fifteen

Nothing really happens for the next two hours.

Well, stuff happens, but nothing finishes. The cops surround the restaurant, helicopters circle overhead, satellite news trucks show up and start doing live remotes—it's a media circus in no time. But as far as Scooter and Adonna and Jimmy—nothing. They refuse to respond to phone calls or bullhorned instructions, so it's a standoff.

A grouchy state patrol captain interviewed us, but Erica and I had enough sense not to give too much information. We didn't lie, actually, it was more like we didn't volunteer any more than the vaguest "We're not sures" to his questions. He had problems with us, I could tell, but he was too busy in the moment to bother us. I'm sure we'll have some hell to pay when this is all over.

"So you know these people?" he asked.

"Just one of them," I answered. "James Biffman." I explained how he called and Erica and I came down to see what was going on with him, that we were worried about him, *blahblahblah*. Sort of a lie, but not important enough to get me in trouble with God.

I hope, anyway.

Erica and I lean against the hood of a state patrol car and wait. Our mini-van is going to be evidence, so we'll have to drive home in the beer truck. But we can't leave. Not yet.

"Are you praying for them, Erica?" I ask.

She stares at the restaurant's front door. Her face is impossible to read. "No."

"You should be, you know. Prayer is the only thing way we can help right now. If God—"

"Eric?"

"Yes?"

"Shut the fuck up."

She walks away.

My wife hates me. Scooter and Jimmy and Adonna have taken her from me. I hesitate. Should I let this pass?

No!

"Erica!" I run after her. She's by the side of the interstate, watching the traffic roar by. The blast of wind from each passing semi hits us like a wave; it's hard to keep from being knocked over. "I can't let this stand! You've got to forget about those people and come home!"

"I *am* coming home, Eric! You've won, okay? I'll be the good little wife, I'll stay home and take care of the kids and the house, I'll go to bible study with Pastor Ernie and I'll do all that meek little holy housewife horseshit that's so important to you...I'll do it all. But just don't expect me to *FUCKING ENJOY IT, OKAY?!*" A triple semi shrieks past and blasts his airhorns for no apparent reason other than to be obnoxious.

"What's happened to you?" I ask. Maybe it's the wind, the dry air, the dust, who knows, but my eyes are watering to the point of tears rolling down my cheeks. I roughly wipe them away. If Erica notices, she doesn't say anything.

"I woke up, Eric."

"That doesn't make any sense."

"For all these years I just quit. I did what you wanted, I forgot about any idea of living my life."

"That's not true! You wanted—"

"I didn't know what I wanted. We got married when we were babies, then I started *having* babies, and then it was all over for me. I don't blame you, not really. I let myself slip away. And now I'm sorry. I know it's too late to change my life, but for a few days I saw how things were outside. Scooter understood."

"He killed somebody! Is that what you want?!" She's talking nonsense, like she's on drugs or something. I don't understand how to deal with this. Or her.

She sighs and shrugs. "You'll never understand. Haven't you ever wanted out, Eric? Haven't you ever wished your life wasn't the way it was, trapped with me and the kids and the business? Haven't you ever just wanted to get in the car and drive away? Go native?"

"No."

"You're lying. You wouldn't be human if you haven't thought about it. Admit it, you've had thoughts about hitting the road, hooking up with some wild twenty-year-old waitress, getting crazy."

"No!"

"Then you're not normal. Jesus has turned your brain to mush."

"That's blasphemy," I say, more out of habit than belief.

"Whatever, Eric," Erica says. "I'll come back, I'll do everything you want. But I won't do one thing."

"What?" I ask, dreading what's coming.

"I won't believe anymore. I'll make sure the kids believe, I won't mess with them. And to everybody looking in from the outside, I'll pretend everything is just like it was and my little trip down here was a kind of mental burp. They'll cluck-cluck that I had a hysterical nervous breakdown, they'll pray for me and you and the kids, and after a few months they'll forget. Pastor Ernie will keep a close eye on me, probably give me some of his bogus life advice—as if the bozo knows anything about the world other than installing garbage disposals and snaking sewer lines—and I'll nod and tell him I'm praying day and night for forgiveness. But you need to know, Eric. From now on, I don't believe it. If there's a god, great. If not, that's great too."

I'm horrified. I can't speak, this is the ultimate in blaspheming the Lord! *Please, Jesus, give me the strength to respond to this sin! Help me bring her back!*

I wait, but Jesus doesn't answer. It's another life test He's giving me. How do I respond?

"I don't think," I finally say, "that I can tolerate those conditions."

"You don't have any choice, Eric. If you want a mother for the children, if you want a happy little wife to show the world, then you're gonna have to face the fact that deep down inside I'm a godless woman, and that maybe, just maybe, I'll take off again. I'm not saying that I will...but you never know."

We stand by the interstate in the hot wind, and there's nothing left to say. I've never seen this look on Erica's face before. It's strength, it's mastery. She's won a game and now she's taunting me. I remember the expression from back in my football days, when somebody would whip us and we'd be shaking hands after the game. They'd be saying, "Good game," but their expressions were filled with bitter victory. They'd stepped on us, and it felt good. I suppose I looked the same way when we won. It's just that you don't want to see that nasty expression on your wife's face. It means that home life isn't going to be a whole lot of fun.

"I'm sorry," I say before I realize I'm saying it. "I'm not a bad person."

"No. You're just you. This whole mess is because of me. I was trying to live through Scooter, and now he's in a jam. And so are you. So go ahead and blame me. I do."

I'm about to respond when the gunfire starts.

As shootouts go, it's pretty brief.

We watch from behind a police van. Somebody inside the restaurant shot first, and the police responded with a cascade of shots and tear gas. Sporadic *popopops* went back and forth, and now there's silence. Tear gas smoke pours out of the restaurant's broken windows, and a buzzy neon "*Dos Equis*" sign blinks in the haze, hanging forlornly where a window used to be.

"Please come out," Erica whispers.

I say quick prayers, and wish I could encourage Erica to pray, but I suppose that's dicey right now.

The cops are on the bullhorns, demanding surrender and promising safety.

No response.

"How long will they wait?" Erica asks.

"I don't know. I've only seen stuff like this on TV. I don't know how they do it in real life."

Nothing happens for a half-hour, and then, suddenly, more gunshots blast from inside. The police fire back, the front door flies open, and Scooter rushes out. At first I think he's coming out to surrender, but then, to my everlasting horror, I see that he's running, gun blazing, just like Butch and Sundance—and you know what happened to them.

And now, it's strange, but things really do go slow motion. I see bullets rip into Scooter's body, he's zippered with shots, his gun (where did he get a gun?) goes flying, he jerks spasmodically like a puppet, *blamblamblam*, and I think he's dead before he hits the ground.

I grab Erica to protect her, to cover her eyes, but she won't let me. She watches her best friend, her all-time buddy, bleeding and still in the red New Mexico dust. She doesn't cry, she doesn't really react, which surprises me...and now, finally, I get it.

Erica always loved him. She should've married Scooter, not me. How come we make the wrong choices and then live with them? She never really wanted to follow the Lord, to teach our children. She didn't know what she wanted, but that wasn't it.

And as Scooter Biffman, former sports reporter, lies dead in front of us, I wonder if Erica wishes she were in his place. Scooter took his walk on the wild side, and a few minutes ago he committed suicide. I'm saddened that he'll never meet Jesus, that he'll spend eternity burning in the flames of hell. But he made the choice. And he *did* have a choice.

So does Erica. I hope she makes the right one.

"I'm sorry, Erica," I whisper.

And now the tears begin. No sobs, no heaving drama, just silent tears sliding down her face. She takes my hand, and I realize that our lives are forever changed. I hope we can make it work.

But I'm not sure.

Nothing happens for another hour. Scooter lies peacefully in the hot, late afternoon sun. The cops are more than willing to wait out Jimmy and Adonna, especially since it's obvious that people are willing to die. Finally, for no reason that I can see, Adonna appears at the door with her hands up. The cops order her out, she flops face down on the dirt with her hands behind her head, and then Jimmy comes out and does the same. Oddly, knowing what trouble they're in, neither looks very frightened or bothered. Their eyes are puffy and red, and they're coughing and gagging from the tear gas.

The cops roughly search them for weapons, cuff them, and then drag them away to waiting cars. Jimmy spots us through his fat-slit eyes as they're pushing him into the cop car, and he gives Erica the most intimate smile. I don't ever want to know what went on between them. Erica waves, and then Adonna and Jimmy are gone.

News reporters wrap up the story, and their satellite trucks drive off. The county coroner picks up Scooter after they've photographed him from every angle. They zip him up in a body bag, drop him on a gurney, load him up.

And he's gone.

We have to wait around, get interview by more cops and investigators, and finally, long after darkness has settled on the red rock desert, they let us leave. We'll have to testify at various trials, give more statements and explanations, and when we get home we'll need to lawyer up. But I think we'll end up okay.

Legally, at least.

But as for Erica.

I just don't know.

I hope prayer will bring her back to me. Will stop her restlessness. Will keep her from looking back and wishing things had been different. That she had made different choices.

I don't know.

I just don't know....

Erica

Chapter Sixteen

It seems like a dream.

It's trite, I know. But that's the way it seems. The reality is too much, I just can't get my brain around it. So it sits there, popping up twenty, fifty, a hundred times a day.

Like a dream. But I know it's not, and I can't change anything.

It's killing me.

Time has passed. Scooter's buried. Jane didn't even bother coming. Eric and I picked up Crystal and took her to the funeral, but she seemed bored and was in a hurry to get to soccer practice.

All our kids were there, of course, along with everybody in the church. Eric insisted that Pastor Ernie do the graveside service—since Scooter didn't have any religious beliefs—so Scooter Biffman was buried in a godly fashion. He would've laughed at that. A few of Scooter's old buddies from the newspaper showed up, but between them and my family, that was about it.

Scooter's parents had died years before in a car accident, he was an only child, and we couldn't find any other relatives to notify. There are probably some out there, but if we couldn't track them down, they probably weren't too important to Scooter anyway.

As they lowered Scooter into the hole, I tried hard to cry. But I couldn't. Because I knew he was better off.

I found myself wishing I was in the casket.

Sick, isn't it? But that's the way I felt. Eric has been pouty since we got back from New Mexico, and I can't say as I blame him. After all, he's thinking the worst about me. I'm sure he's positive I had sex with Handsome Jimmy, that I robbed minimarts and played Bonnie and Clyde all over the southwest. I haven't bothered to tell him otherwise. I know I should, but I'm too weary.

I need to do something about this. I go through my days teaching the kids, being the mom, missing Scooter—

And thinking about what I might have done.

That day that Eric walked in the Mexican restaurant, I'd almost come to a decision. I'd almost—*almost*—decided to stay on the road with them. I know, I know, I thought I'd decided to go home. I'd told Eric I was coming back, I'd told Scooter I was going home, I'd made up my mind.

But then...I got to the highway. I turned on the road, looked at the sky, the scenery. The life I was returning to...as much as I loved the kids, as much as I felt the responsibility...I didn't want to go back. Not really. I was a selfish scum. No doubt about it.

I found Handsome Jimmy and Adonna. They were getting ready to go on a robbery spree. Why? Because they could. We ate Mexican food, I listened to them. Adonna was a nasty piece of work, but considering her life it wasn't surprising. But Handsome Jimmy. I couldn't avoid being captivated by him. As they talked and planned and plotted I watched Handsome Jimmy, such a charmer, all that good brain being wasted, but....

He was happy.

I think he had some weird love for Adonna still, even though she was ugly and bitter. That showed me he had a good heart. As for the illegal, well, I convinced myself that I could rationalize my way around it. Stupid, I know.

But I convinced myself that I would join them.

Then Eric and Scooter showed up, and it was over.

I've tried to feel guilt for what happened to Scooter, and I suppose I do have some, but he made his choices. I set the thing in motion with my lame idea to look up Adonna (that seems so naïve and innocent now; finding a high school crush—what *was* I thinking?), but Scooter jumped on and finished it the way he wanted. He could've turned back any time, and he almost did. But then he decided to make the change permanent, if short, and that's the way it went. I can't fault him for that. And I won't blame myself.

Eric does, though. He doesn't say anything, but I know he's almost afraid of me now. Of what I might be capable of.

The prayers and counseling started in earnest the minute we got home. Idiot Pastor Ernie chucked and huffled and spewed bible chapter and verse at me, I demurely pretended to listen, nodded when appropriate, and daydreamed my way through my return to salvation. Eric has been in a prayer frenzy, and he's moving his lips so much all the time mumbling Jesus pleas that he looks like one of those crazy homeless people you see at the bus station.

And the kids....

The little ones are just glad Mommie's back, the older ones look at me, wondering. They know enough about life—even though we've sheltered them with home-schooling and religious brainwashing—to know that you can't count on people. On parents. On moms who take off and run with criminals.

It's strange. The way they look at me, I'm almost proud to have planted doubt in their heads. I love them all so much, so fiercely, that I can't understand why I'd be pleased to expose them to human deceit and treachery. Maybe I think it'll make them stronger. I hope that by seeing their mother having doubts, wanting something different, that they won't be afraid when their chances come. I don't want them to end up like me.

God, I don't want that.

I've talked to Handsome Jimmy a few times. Eric doesn't know, of course. And it's going to stay that way.

The first time I called him, he was still in jail down in New Mexico. He'd been charged with a batch of felonies, and he had some outstanding charges for drugs and nastiness from before I met him. They were going to transfer him up to Denver shortly.

"Gonna be doin' some pretty hard time," he chuckled when I spoke to him.

"Are you okay?" I asked stupidly.

"Would you be if you were in my place, Erica?"

"How's Adonna?"

"Dunno. She's on her own now. I think I may have to cut her loose. She always drags me into trouble."

"It's not like you'll have a choice," I said.

"Yep, 'spose so. Don't know of many co-ed prisons."

I hesitated before I asked, but I needed to know. "Why did Scooter do it?"

"You mean go out in a blaze of glory?" I could hear the smile in his voice. I thought it was pretty heartless to be smiling about Scooter's dying, but, strangely, I found myself smiling too.

"It was funny," Handsome Jimmy continued. "We were tryin' to decide what to do, if there was a way out of the pickle that holy-roller husband of yours got us into, and we'd pretty much decided the game was over."

"Even Adonna?"

"Yeah. Even crazy Adonna. I think she was scared. Never seen that before. So old Scoot tells us he'll go out the front, take the heat, and we can sneak out the back. I tried to tell him it didn't matter, the place was surrounded, but he wouldn't listen to me. He went on and on about if he could survive a lightning strike he could survive anything, then he starts the giggling shit, next thing I know he takes my gun, yells somethin' about bein' free, and he's out the door getting shot. Strange fellow, old Scooter. Liked him, though."

"He knew he was going to get killed."

"Seems like. Didn't really care, though. That impressed me."

After that we chatted amiably, and it felt nice. I like talking to Handsome Jimmy.

"You back in the Jesus saddle with that husband of yours?" he asked.

"Yes. No. I'm pretending."

"Shouldn't do that, Erica. Don't know you all that well, but I know you enough to be able to see that the pretending shit won't work. Oughta be honest with him."

"I can't," I whispered.

"Suit yourself," Handsome Jimmy said. "But you know I'm right."

The other times I've talked to Handsome Jimmy we haven't gotten into the deep, "What's the matter with Erica?" questions. Just chitchat.

He's on trial now, and I've decided not to talk to him anymore. It's not good for me. I'm upset afterwards, and I'm not sure why. Maybe I'm a little in love with the guy, I don't know. I don't think so. I had a stupid crush on him at the beginning, but that's gone. I think.

I don't know for sure. I don't know anything anymore.

Eric comes home from work tonight in a foul mood. I've had a tough day of whiny kids.

Ain't life grand?

"The hamburger was a little pink," Eric says after dinner. Needle, needle. Erica, the incompetent wife and mother, poisoning her family with killer ground chuck.

I don't answer. The Tuesday night shift of dishwashing kids works noisily in the kitchen as Eric and I sit at opposite ends of the dining room table. I hear the usual noise and disorder of the non-working kids playing, goofing, being children in the rest of the house. Sometimes, the noise soothes and pleases me. Not tonight. Tonight I'm annoyed. Too much. Too much....

"Have a good day?" Eric asks.

"Yes. You?"

"Sure. Another day, another ocean of beer. It's nice to know I'm in the business of ruining people's lives."

Oh boy, here we go. Eric gets into self-pitying moods sometimes, blaming himself for every alcoholic or drunk driving accident that ever happened. I usually talk him out of his funk, telling him it's not his fault, people have personal choice, all that. But I don't have the energy tonight. Besides, I'm not all that sure about personal choice anymore. Sometimes you do things and you can't help yourself. I've found that this whole disaster with Scooter has made me less judgmental toward human weakness.

"Aren't you going to say anything?" Eric asks.

"What would you like me to say? 'Everything's okay, you're a good person?' There, that make you feel better?"

Eric sighs. "We can't go on like this, Er."

"I know."

"We should pray together."

"Go ahead."

"We need to do it together. Pastor Ernie says—"

I leave the table.

I lock myself in the bathroom and cry. There's nothing else to do. I need help, I need rescue, I need—

I need to leave.

When clarity hits you, when understanding and self-knowledge and truth finally take over, it both hurts and pleases. When I thought the words, "I need to leave", everything changed. I felt peace, calm. Like the way a prayer is supposed to make you feel—but never has for me.

I know now what I have to do. The tears stop, and the calm, oh, it's so nice, so relaxing, *the truth shall set you free!*

I go through the house and kiss the children one by one. Not unusual, I kiss the sweet little darlings all the time. They don't notice anything odd, the little ones just accept a mommy kiss as always, the older ones squirm or accuse me of being a nerd, but that's okay. One last kiss is what I must have before I do this.

I should pack some clothes, toiletries, something. But I don't. I have to go.

Eric's in the family room. The TV is on to *Jeopardy*, but Eric's not listening. His lips move in whispery prayer. I should tell him, I should say something.

I start to move, then stop. I see the back of his head over the chair, his reflection on the TV screen. He stops praying. He knows I'm there, but he pretends not to.

Silence between us. The TV fills the void. So much to say, but nobody's going to say anything.

I sigh. *Goodbye, Eric,* I think.

And then I leave.

The minivan starts up and idles roughly. It hasn't run right since the cops gave it back to us. I think they sabotaged it. The garage door grinds open, and I back into the driveway.

It's a clear night. As the garage door closes I look up at the sky. Stars. So many stars.

I'll miss the children. If there's a hell that's where I'm headed, because mothers who desert their children are the lowest of the low. But I know that Eric and his mom and the church will take care of them. Maybe Eric can marry some obedient little religious woman. She'll do a fine job of finishing the task of raising my children.

Guilt. So much guilt. But freedom. That's the urge I follow, because it's the strongest of all. Scooter came to understand that when he was on the road. It took a lightning bolt and death to free him. I hope it'll be easier for me.

I'm already halfway there, because I've made the choice. It's final, it's forever, there's no going back.

I have no idea what I'll do, where I'll go. But as I put the minivan into reverse, back into the street, and drive away from my life forever, the exhilaration is like a drug. I'm smiling, crying, laughing, gasping, ohmygod, the power of taking charge, it's, it's....

Scooter. All the years of dullness, suburbia, of cozy friendship, who would've thought it would come to this? Scooter dead, me running away. But it had to be. It began the night I opened the old high school yearbook and Adonna smiled out at us. And now, it's up to me to finish what Scooter started.

Free.

I'm driving. Where?

I don't know.

But that's okay.

Because now I'm tasting sweet freedom.

I'm a runaway.

www.ingramcontent.com/pod-product-compliance
Lightning Source LLC
LaVergne TN
LVHW010611100826
845148LV00014B/2919

* 9 7 8 0 9 7 2 8 2 1 8 4 1 *